NEVER
TOO OLD FOR
Fairy
Tales

MELISSA JOHN

First paperback edition September 2023

Book design by Getcovers
Edited by Chloe Cran

ISBN: 9798854085793 (paperback)

www.melissajohn.co.uk

Please Note

This book was written in the UK, where some spelling, grammar and word usage will vary from US English.

Dedicated to

My son
You are my light.

My mumma
Thank you for... everything.
(At least my mum thinks I'm funny).

My husband
Thank you for rescuing this manuscript from the bin (several times).
You are the wind beneath my wings. My hero. What a mighty good man.

Kim Namjoon, Kim Seokjin, Min Yoongi, Jung Hoseok, Park Jimin, Kim Taehyung, Jeon Jungkook, and fellow BTS ARMY
Thank you for supporting me through the long nights, believing in me, giving me courage and hope, and for being my inspiration. *Gamsahamnida. Apobangpo.*

Playlist

Behind the story... BTS – my inspiration. This playlist sets the mood and stirs the imagination. Enjoy the songs that bring *Never Too Old for Fairy Tales* to life. *Borahae*.

YouTube
youtube.com/@melissajohnauthor

Spotify
bit.ly/SpotifyNTOFFT

Whalien 52
Set Me Free – Jimin
Mikrokosmos
Dimple
So What?
Young Forever
Butterfly
Awake
Zero o'clock
Fake Love
Blue and Grey
Lost
Epiphany

Pied Piper
Not Today
Wishing on a Star
Love Myself
Dionysus
(Burning Up) Fire
Heartbeat
The Truth Untold
Singularity
Yours – Jin
Tonight – Jin
Still With You – JK
Life Goes On

Contents

Part 1: Never Too Old For Fairy Tales

PART ONE

Never Too Old For Fairy Tales

Dream - Discover - Delight

'Are you ready for the most magical week of your life, ladies?' Nanny Prim bustles down the aisle of our executive tour bus, reminding me of Mary Poppins with her cheery disposition and rosy cheeks. She adjusts her hat, ruffles her skirt, and I half-expect her to burst into song.

Lexi squeals and jumps up from her seat. 'I am! Are we nearly there?'

'Not far now!' Nanny Prim beams.

Lexi's eyes widen as she grasps my arm, bouncing with each bump along the long, winding drive out to the middle of nowhere. 'I hope there's a castle with a moat and drawbridge and a real dragon… and a pegasus.'

As I take a quick glimpse at the golden glow of dusk settling over the deserted countryside, my only wish right now is to stretch my restless legs. And have something to take my mind off the *Spoonful of Sugar* earworm stuck in my head since seeing our practically perfect resort chaperone.

I ease back into the plush seat and let my eyes drift closed while Lexi chatters about all the legendary creatures that may await. I still can't believe my luck in being specially selected to review a luxury holiday resort – all expenses paid! Me! Out of all the other writers at the magazine. And honestly, this break from real life couldn't come at a better time for my daughter and me.

Who wouldn't want to get lost in a fairy-tale wonderland for a while?

'It won't be real magic though, will it?' Lexi whispers, her breath warming my ear.

'Maybe she means it will be so much fun, it will feel magical.' I put my arm around her shoulders and give her a squeeze. 'I can't wait to have an adventure with my favourite child.'

'I'm your only child!' Lexi giggles and pokes my ribs before gasping with sudden inspiration. 'It might be like living inside one of our favourite princess movies.'

Ah yes, the warbling soundtrack of our lives on eternal repeat for as long as my mum-brain can remember.

Lexi snuggles close, her head resting on my shoulder and the familiar scent of her floral shampoo tickling my nose. I wish I could bottle moments like these before my tween becomes a teen and cuddles might become as rare as her tidying her room.

She tilts her face up to me, blue eyes no longer round and childlike but almond-shaped like her dad's. Her brows furrow into a frown as she bites her lip. 'Mum, I... I think I might be getting too old for fairy tales. Are you cross with me?'

My heart clenches at this sweet sorrow – another sign my baby's growing up too fast.

'No, darling. Of course not. It's a pity we all grow out of believing in magic.' Staring out at the rolling hills fading into black silhouettes, I'm crying inside, *Nooo! Stay little as long as possible! Being an adult is exhausting!* But I understand. Nine's an awkward age, caught between clinging to the last shreds of little-girl wonder and longing to be grown up.

'Don't you believe in magic then?' She sits up, her surprise catching me off guard.

'I would if little birds opened our curtains in the morning and woodland creatures cooked our dinner each night.'

Lexi giggles, her petite frame quivering against me. 'What about fairy tales? You must believe in happily ever afters? You and Dad have been together forever.'

I twiddle her unruly chestnut curls, stuck for an answer when I can't remember the last time I felt happy with Ben. Sadly, our marriage is beyond being magically saved by a bit of fairy dust.

'I wish Dad wasn't too busy to come on holiday with us.'

'Hmm.' So he said. More like he was pissed off I'd be working and he might have to *babysit*. Hackles raised, I pull Lexi's magazine from our carrier bag of snacks to save me from any more awkward questions.

This opportunity is amazing and I'm not going to let his lack of support ruin it. I need this to go well. I have to prove to the chief ed I can do more than review local kids' days out. It's embarrassing to get to this age still waiting for my first ever promotion. I could do with finally getting some validation. And I really need that pay rise. At least then I'd have some options.

A text notification sounds, and I dig around in my handbag for my phone. Is the office hassling me already?

'Oh! It's a message from your dad.'

'What does it say?'

'He wants to know where I keep my cleaning stuff.' *My* cleaning stuff. What a cheek. Lexi sniggers.

'I can't imagine Dad doing the cleaning!'

I scroll down to the rest of his message.

I had to get a woman to cover for you

Cover for me? I re-read his message, seething more and more with each word I imagine being shouted. I'm not his maid! Is that all he sees me as? Why can't a grown-ass man look after himself for a few days?

I can feel my indignation turning to self-pity. *I* could have done with someone to help *me* out all these years. I could have gone back to my career when Lexi started school. The familiar burning inside my chest is back, and it hurts to breathe in. I could have been doing something I was good at instead of failing at being a domestic goddess. Would it kill him to consider *me* for once?

Being a quiet, subservient little housewife was never how I imagined my life would turn out. God, I had even convinced myself that would make him appreciate me again. I never thought that when I got to my forties my life would feel so small or lonely or pitiful. Where did I go so wrong?

My phone chimes again with another message from Ben. My heart is beating so fast it could burst. This better be him wishing his daughter a fun holiday and wishing me good luck. At least then I would know he gives a shit about us.

She needs the spare key
What have you done with it this time?

I swallow back the nausea as I switch off my phone and chuck it back in my bag. What I would give to slam down the phone like in the olden days. I have loved my husband, but sometimes I wish he was buried under the patio. Still, as always, it's better that I put up and shut up rather than get into another argument.

The bus pulls over, and I am grateful for the interruption to my thoughts. Nanny Prim gets up as the doors open.

'Are we there yet?' Lexi asks for the millionth time.

'I don't think so.' I strain to see some civilisation through the window. 'It looks like another empty bus station.'

'I'm getting bored,' Lexi whines. 'We can't even play I Spy now that it's getting dark.'

A cute girl who looks about four years old climbs on board, her blonde pigtails tied with royal-blue ribbons that match her party dress.

Lexi squeezes my arm and whispers, 'I didn't know we were supposed to dress up.'

As I turn to face her, I catch sight of my scraggly, dark-blonde ponytail reflected in the bus window and try to smooth down all the wispy hairs that have escaped.

The two of us squirm in our regular t-shirts, leggings, and trainers, and we both sink a little lower in our seats.

The little girl's mother bursts onto the bus, designer logos plastered all over her coat and bag. A shorter, unassuming man follows in her shadow. Our compact space is suddenly overwhelmed by the woman's sickly perfume and over-enthusiastic plummy babbling.

Lexi looks at me wide-eyed. 'Will this place be posh?'

'It could be, so let's hope they'll have a gigantic chocolate fountain.' We both giggle at the thought.

'Dad said we would have to sell our house to come here normally.'

'I'm not sure he was joking.'

A young couple comes aboard next. The man carefully cradles a sleeping toddler in his arms and the woman trails behind, holding a *Just Married* balloon. We smile at each other as they walk past to their seats.

I sigh as a wave of envy creeps over me. Young and in love, happily starting out on their journey together.

Fools, I huff quietly to myself. They're smiling now, but it won't last.

Fine. I admit that was a bit harsh, but I can't help feeling bitter. I miss the days when Ben and I were happy in the beginning. I feel a pang of sadness and despair at how things have turned out. How lovely it would have been for the three of us to take this trip together as a loving family.

But now I can't wait for a week away from him constantly putting me down. Particularly when I'm perfectly capable of being my own worst critic.

As the bus rumbles onwards, Nanny Prim's melodious voice calls for everyone's attention. 'Ladies and gentlemen, prepare to experience the world of your dreams. A magical resort where fairy tales come alive.'

'This is going to be the best holiday ever!' Lexi's face lights up with a huge grin and bubbly laughter that makes my heart swell. Fairy-tale magic is just what we both need.

'It sounds amazing, doesn't it?'

How perfect would it be to run off into a fairy tale and never look back? We could escape the prince who turned into a frog and snuggle up by the fire in our cosy gingerbread house in the woods. And me and Lex would live happily ever after.

Nanny Prim appears with a large pink gift box for Lexi, who stares open-mouthed before managing to whisper a thank you. She hurriedly pulls the ribbon and lifts the lid, unleashing a dozen mini helium balloons and a flurry of confetti. Squealing in delight, she shakes out her hair and scatters the shredded tissue paper until she pulls out a teddy bear dressed as a princess, complete with Lexi's name embroidered on its dress.

Lexi gives her new bear a big squeeze. 'Welcome to Fairy-Tale Wonderland!'

'Princess Bear talks!' Lexi gasps in awe. 'Oh Mum, I love her!'

I take out the card. 'It says that when you press her paw, she will tell you about the kids' club activities and give you special messages for your holiday. That's so cute!'

Lexi presses the bear's paw again and again, listening to all the messages until I want to pull its cute little head off.

'Lex, remember that child was asleep.'

She stops pressing and fiddles with the bear's crown. Thank you, sleeping child. You've saved me from a teddy-induced migraine and rescued the bear from being thrown out of the window.

I rip open a golden envelope from the box and pull out a beautifully handmade card that says *Tickets* on the front. Inside, the swirly gold lettering reads *Escape from reality at our exclusive fairy-tale-themed resort. We look forward to welcoming you very soon.* The words *Dream – Discover – Delight* are ornately penned along the bottom.

I lean back in my seat, clutching the card to my chest. A whole week of escaping from reality. Just like fairy-tales used to be my escape when I was a little girl. They transported me out of my miserable, unstable family life into lands of hopes and dreams. And even though there were granny-eating wolves and bone-grinding giants, the goodies always won and there was always a happy ending. If only real life was that simple.

Nerves flutter in my stomach, crowding out my excitement. I wonder if they make reviewers sleep in a shed somewhere remote? Why did they pick *me* to review the resort anyway? What if my article isn't good enough to warrant our free holiday?

Heart racing, I fan myself with the card and wave it in front of Lexi, who looks a bit flushed. A symbol on the back catches my eye: a phone in a red ring with a line through it.

We have a 'no phones or cameras' policy in our resort. We have discreet professional photographers on-site to capture your fun and will present you with a photobook to take home at the end of your stay.

This news is both odd and terrifying! I can't remember how to survive without a phone in my hand. I drop the card into my lap, fingertips drumming a restless rhythm. A whole week of no social media, no work emails and calls... Actually, that sounds really quite wonderful. But what if I need to urgently Google what size fairy wings a human would need to fly or how to tell if a witch put a curse on you as a baby? And no camera? What on earth is that all about?

The bus begins to climb a steep hill and as I look up, I accidentally catch the loud woman's eye.

'Your first visit?'

She twists to face me. Her salt-and-pepper hair, overly lacquered into probably the same flick from the 80s, seems to turn a second after her head.

'Ye–'

'It's what, Charles? Our seventh, eighth time?' Charles, sitting on a seat in front by himself, doesn't even try to get a word in edgeways. 'Oh, you'll love it!' Her voice carries to the back of the bus, and I'm surprised she doesn't wake the child behind us. 'I hope you like having fun! They'll have you up on stage, in singing competitions, playing team games, salsa dancing, bingo... It's a hoot!'

'Sounds great!' I force a smile, hoping to mask my growing anxiety. This woman clearly has a different idea of what is magical and fun. I am tone deaf with two clumsy left feet – no way am I doing competitions. And being on stage is my worst nightmare.

'I can't wait!' Lexi chirps. It might sound like holiday camp hell to me, but it warms my heart to see her smile again. I grab her hand and give it an encouraging squeeze, joining in with her excitement. Maybe it's too late for things to change for me, but I hate how she's been suffering from all the tension at home.

She always loved performing her made-up song and dance routines at home. Before Ben started stropping and shouting all the time. When home was still our safe and cosy little space to relax and play.

'We're here for my birthday, aren't we, Charles?' The woman's voice lowers as she mouths, 'It's my big four-o. Can you believe it?' She chuckles.

'How lovely. Happy birthday.'

She's younger than me! I hope my face doesn't show my shock; if she'd said fifty, I wouldn't have been surprised. I don't look that old, do I? My fingertips search for laughter lines around my eyes. She looks so mature, like a proper adult who's got her life sorted out. Whereas, I just seem to be ageing like milk – getting sour and chunky.

'Let's have a bus singalong to get us all in the holiday mood!' she says, appointing herself as life and soul of the party. I duck behind the headrest, out of her view.

In the nick of time, Nanny Prim claps her hands for our attention. 'Welcome to Fairy-Tale Wonderland,' she announces dramatically, her hand sweeping to the bus windows. There's a faint glow in the distance. As the bus nears the top of the hill, the glow becomes brighter and wider. The bus comes to a stop at the hill's crest and its lights turn off, allowing us to see through the darkness.

'Behold.' Nanny Prim beams.

My jaw drops. There is stunned silence, quickly followed by gasps of wonder and delight. Then... cheering and clapping from Mrs Life-and-Soul-of-the-Party.

The entire valley dazzles far into the distance, as if a rainbow has burst into a sea of shimmering diamonds. A huge palace dominates the centre, its tall towers glowing bright purple against the dark evening sky. The surrounding buildings twinkle like glittering gems, their lights casting a myriad of vibrant colours across the sprawling forests.

We really are being transported to a magical land of dreams! Perhaps we really will be living in a fairy tale!

Lexi slips her hand into mine, and my heart skips a beat as I glance down to see the awe etched on her little face. She gasps, her eyes doubling in size and sparkling as much as the magnificent view. She grips my hand tightly, her body trembling with excitement.

As the bus rolls on, we fall back into our seats, buzzing with anticipation. What magical adventures do we have in store?

Within moments, Lexi turns towards me, making a strange guttural noise. 'Mum, I think...' She claps her hand over her mouth. And then she vomits all over our legs.

'Oh, my poor baby.' I push Lexi's hair back out of her face as the wetness seeps through to my thighs. Excited butterflies in her tummy have obviously not mixed well with bumpy roads and too much orange soda. With nothing else to hand, I use my fingers to wipe a string of goo hanging from her lips. Thankfully, Princess Bear remains unscathed, but still, I'm not sure this is how a magical experience is supposed to begin.

Before I can move, Nanny Prim pops up beside us.

'Whoopsadaisy! Here, my lovely, you take these wipes, and I'll get this little one cleaned up.'

I nod gratefully, and she whisks Lexi off to the on-board bathroom while I clean myself and try not to heave at the smell.

'Poor girl,' sympathises Mrs Life-and-Soul-of-the-Party. 'If she's feeling better, will I see you both for *Sunrise Chanting Meditation* in the morning?'

The thought of her being quiet enough to meditate, or me chanting – at sunrise – makes me laugh out loud. I appreciate her attempt to take my mind off my unfortunate situation. I look up, grinning. She pretends to be serious, which makes me laugh more. But she doesn't laugh along with me... I think she's deadly serious.

Lexi returns clean and fresh, with a great big smile and wearing a resort t-shirt long enough to pass as a dress. Nanny Prim hands me a bag of stinky, sodden clothes, then sanitises our seats, finishing with a spritz of fresh citrus scents. Wow! I may have to kidnap this amazing woman and take her home with me.

'I love Nanny P,' Lexi coos. 'She made up a song about putting a smile back on my face.'

'I'm glad you're feeling better.' I pull her into a big hug. 'Give me a warning next time!'

Lexi pouts. 'Sorry, Mum.'

'You don't have to apologise, my darling. I know sometimes you get sick when you're extra excited.'

'Nanny P said she was going to be my nanny for the whole week. Isn't that awesome? Did you know a nanny is like an aunty or babysitter? Her real name is Primrose, but she said I could call her Nanny P.'

'Aww, sounds like you've made a friend already.' I love to see her looking so happy. She rests her head on my shoulder, and we both close our eyes. I try to relax, but my legs feel sticky and gross.

After a long, winding journey towards the lights, the bus slows to a halt. 'Here we are!' trills Nanny P. 'I hope you have a magical stay and all your dreams come true. The hostesses will show you to your rooms.'

I stand and stretch my stiff body, and my poor old bones creak and crack as we make our way off the bus. A group of attractive young women dressed in smart pink skirt suits are there to greet us – and they all curtsy. I haven't seen anyone curtsy since I danced around a maypole at primary school. I respond with a graceless half-curtsy, attempting to pull my orange-vomit-stained leggings out to the sides. My cheeks burn.

One of the pink women approaches and curtsies again, smiling sweetly. 'Cally Jackson? Lexi?'

How did she know it was us? Oh no, do we stand out as the freeloaders? I look at the state of us both. Yes, yes we do. No designer labels and pearls here, just vomit and a free t-shirt.

'That's us.' I nudge Lexi – it's her turn to curtsy back, which she does with dramatic flair.

'Welcome to Fairy-Tale Wonderland. My name is Thalia, I will be your personal assistant this week.'

I shuffle awkwardly, trying to hide the supermarket logo on my plastic bag while becoming distracted by the faint clip-clopping of hooves. Then, as she is speaking, my attention is taken by a glow far behind her.

Rounding a bend, the glow transforms into a glittering carriage led by white horses in feathered headdresses and carrying none other than Cinderella! My heart leaps at seeing my all-time favourite fairy-tale character, her golden hair and iconic blue gown illuminated by the carriage lanterns.

Some might just see a woman in costume, but to me, Cinderella is the embodiment of all my childhood dreams. I try to get a better view, but I don't want to appear rude to the woman in pink talking to us.

'If there is anything you need, I will do my very best to help.'

'Thank you.' I drag my focus back to her and smile. 'So sorry, what did you say your name was?'

'Thalia, your personal assistant.' She smiles and gracefully nods.

Looking around, I see that none of the other guests appear to have a personal assistant. Is she keeping tabs on us? How awkward. What's going on?

'The bellboys will take your luggage, and I will show you the way. Please follow me.'

We follow as instructed, and I look behind to get another glimpse of Cinderella. Instead, I get a brief view of Prince Charming. My knees go weak at the sight of his regal attire and chiseled jaw. Oh my goodness! He is *Drop. Dead. Gorgeous.* I'm dying to go back to see them properly, but I'm already lagging behind and I don't want to get lost. Lexi is skipping alongside Thalia, and I jog to catch up.

'How did you know I was Lexi?' she asks, taking hold of Thalia's hand.

'We know all our VIPs, sweetie.'

There must have been some kind of mix-up. VIPs?

High-pitched whistling immediately turns our attention upwards. Above the glowing palace towers that peek over the treetops, a burst of silver light explodes, raining twinkling stars down through the night sky. Lexi gasps, jumping up to throw her arms around my waist. Laughter and applause sounds from the other passengers.

'Mum, this is so awesome! I can't wait to go inside!'

MONDAY

Once Upon a Time

A huge leather book towers before us, as tall as the trees it is nestled between. As I read the gold swirly *'Once Upon a Time'* on the cover, the book slowly opens. A chorus of oohs falls from the lips of the spellbound guests as the book unfolds to reveal an archway of white roses. In gold calligraphy, the left page reads:

Your adventure begins...

'Wow! What an unexpected entrance!' I'm blown away by the spectacle. Even Lexi is speechless – and this is a girl who rarely pauses for breath. Or used to be. Along with several other parents, I automatically reach for my phone to take photos. The hostesses kindly remind us of the no-camera rule and are met with a few low grumbles. This is going to be impossible; I miss my phone already.

The hostesses lead us through the archway to a gorgeous outdoor reception area. We are surrounded by a beautiful display of tree stumps with flickering candles on top and white flowers scattered between. Glasses of champagne are handed to the grown-ups and toadstool-shaped ice-lollies to the children. This review's going to write itself if the rest of the place lives up to its first impressions.

Thalia leads Lexi and me around the corner, bumping into the family in front of us. As they move forward, we also stop in our tracks.

'It's magical!' Lexi whispers, her eyes shining at the sea of twinkling sapphire flower lights and softly lit trees radiating an ethereal blue. I choke back the lump in my throat.

Aromas of candyfloss and doughnuts drift in the gentle breeze, and faint tinkling music meets our ears, as though fairies are playing among us. If fairies *are* real, this is where they would live. I have to agree with Lexi; it does feel like there's magic in the air. The iciest of hearts would thaw here – maybe even a little of mine.

At the end of the mystical blue garden, we find a forest landscape ignited by glittering lights strung high across the tree-lined path.

'It's so pretty.' Lexi gasps, almost finding her voice. It feels wonderful to stroll through nature on this balmy summer evening, especially after being cooped up on the bus for so long. My shoulders begin to relax with each step further away from the outside world.

This hidden world is completely different to the frenzy of crowds and chaos I had expected. Instead of jostling throngs swarming along walkways, we're surrounded only by our small bus load of passengers. There's space and fresh air. This must be what the elite receive for the *exclusive resort* price tag.

The bright lights above give way to little tea lights that guide us. Anticipation builds as the darkness fills with fairy music, getting louder and reaching its crescendo. Our pace quickens and I start to feel like a kid at Christmas. If a unicorn trotted past right now, I wouldn't be surprised. Lexi's bouncing along, about to explode with excitement, while Thalia looks on like a proud parent at our reactions.

Sparkling lights string from trees, merging overhead into a tunnel. Lexi clutches my arm as we emerge into a quaint fairy-tale village square with a village green to one side and on the other... the jaw-dropping, majestic Palace Hotel. We stare up at its tall, pointed towers – it seems like we've walked straight into a bedtime storybook.

'Mum, I think I'm dreaming.' Lexi twirls around, taking in all the wondrous sights.

'Me too, baby girl!' It feels as if I've won the lottery – people like me don't get to go to places like this. It's like all my childhood dreams are coming true. And the dreams I have for my little girl too. I'm so grateful I've been able to bring Lexi to a place like this, especially while she's still young enough to be thrilled by its magic.

My feet stumble over themselves as I turn on the spot for a 360-degree view. This would make a fantastic panoramic photo.

The village square is a hive of activity: guests enjoying cocktails, families playing, bellboys ferrying luggage, and street vendors with ice-cream carts. And then there are larger-than-life fairy-tale characters greeting the new arrivals, with people dressed as fairies and butterflies flitting around in incredible costumes of all colours. The atmosphere is warm and easygoing, as if we're visiting old friends. Just on a grander, more fantastical scale.

'Can I go and meet Snow White?' Lexi pulls at my arm, ready to immerse herself in our magical surroundings.

'I think we have to find where we're staying first, but then we have the whole week to play.' I turn to Thalia to lead us to the broom cupboard accommodation for journalists.

She points up to the hotel. 'You just need to check in at reception.'

'Mum, pleeeease can I go? I'll be good. Promise.'

'I could take Lexi for a few minutes while you get the room keys, if you would like?' Thalia's kind tone and the warmth in her expression put me at ease. Before I've even finished agreeing, Lexi grabs Thalia's hand and zooms off, pulling her new friend behind her. I laugh, watching them run off together.

So far, the resort has exceeded all my expectations, and my mood has lifted already. We're on holiday! In a place that must cost an absolute fortune! And all I have to do is write what I think about it!

I turn towards the Palace Hotel. A glorious fountain of unicorns stands in the front, each spouting colourful illuminated water. Stone staircases curve up each side to the main hotel entrance. It's so photo-worthy.

A cute fairy dressed in silver takes my arm and accompanies me up the steps.

'I'm Gloria. It's wonderful to meet you. Have a magical stay!'

It's hard to maintain my usual tired and grouchy state when I am under the shimmering wing of a fairy. She is exactly how I imagined the fairies at the bottom of my garden when I was a child, just a bit taller.

I hover in the doorway of the hotel. I should be wearing a ballgown or tutu or something more appropriate to enter a fantasy palace. Not vomit-stained leggings, that's for sure. I feel more cackling bog witch than dainty princess. But I put on my big-girl pants and step forward.

I steady myself on the door frame as I take in the lobby, which is grand on a scale I have only seen in movies. Fabulously ostentatious, with possibly the largest, sparkliest chandelier hanging from the painted dome ceiling high above.

An imposing staircase sweeps towards stone archways and balconies on each side of the first floor. It's elegantly decorated with trailing ferns and elaborate white floral displays, with candles on each step. This would make one of those perfect Instagram moments – complete with an inspirational quote and a humble-bragging #feelingblessed.

Seriously though, I do feel blessed. There's just no comparison to the only other family holiday we've had – a grotty caravan in a shabby seaside town, with a grumpy husband to boot. Now we get to see how the other half lives.

I wander around the lobby admiring the decor and all the special touches of this fantasy dreamscape, ending my tour at reception. The desk is carved from an enormous tree trunk and invites my fingers to run along its smooth, polished surface before I fill in a bunch of forms with a squirrel-shaped pen.

Beneath a blossom-covered tree overhanging the end of the desk, a smiling receptionist holds out our room key as though she was already expecting me at that very moment. I turn to see Lexi has already come in and is leaning back against Thalia, mouth agape, staring trance-like at our phenomenal home for the week. Thank you, gods of lucky breaks!

Lexi and I say our thank yous and goodbyes to Thalia and aim for the elevator – sweeping staircases are only for gracefully walking down, not trudging up. We pass the decadent gold throne seating area and hop in the glass elevator to the first floor. We follow the corridor around to Room 121, beep the door open, and step inside.

'Holy sh–'

'Mum, language.'

'Shakira.' My mouth can't fall open any wider as my eyes dart back and forth. Lexi runs inside screaming, 'Is this place for real?' and twirls around with her arms outstretched. We are in a real-life fairy-tale bedroom! A bubblegum-pink retreat with furry rugs, fairy lights, and chandeliers. All for us!

I kick off my shoes, peel off my crunchy leggings, and leap onto my colossal four-poster bed, which is covered with hundreds of fluffy cushions. Spreading out like a starfish, I look up at the pink fabric draped over the gold frame, tied at each corner with garlands of pink roses. 'We're the luckiest girls in the world!'

Squealing in delight, Lexi dives onto her bed – a dreamy hideaway set into the opposite wall.

'I think this is an actual princess's bed!' She peeks out from behind the glittery pink curtains, taking in the twinkling lights woven throughout.

'I've got presents!' She pulls several teddy bear out-fits out of the gift basket. 'More clothes for Princess Bear!' Cuddling her bear with the biggest smile, she emp-ties the basket of all kinds of goodies – slippers, books, chocolates...

'It's like fairy-tale Christmas!'

I peer inside the basket on my bed – handmade soaps, face masks, aromatherapy oils, champagne... I feel so spoiled!

I jump up to explore our room. Our enormous, gleaming en-suite bathroom is bigger than my entire house! White fluffy towels line shelves above a bathtub fit for a queen. Behind the bathroom door hang glossy satin robes adorned with our initials in gold embroidery – monogrammed luxury worthy of royalty! I fall a little more in love with this paradise.

Walking through the deepest shag-pile carpet to-wards the window, I pass our suitcases, which are neatly placed next to the wardrobe – where my clothes will stay. I'll never reach the level of efficiency needed to unpack and hang each item.

I draw back the sumptuous velvet curtains and turn to Lexi with a smirk and exaggerated bow. 'Behold, Prin-cess Alexandra! A royal chamber with vistas of the gilded palace grounds has been bequeathed unto us!'

Lexi shakes her head. 'Mum, don't start acting weird.'

'Cast your gaze upon the wondrous, glistening kingdom.'

'Muuum.' She holds a cushion ready to fire. I look at my bed: plenty of cushion ammunition... But our impending pillow fight is interrupted by a knock at the door.

'Ooh, visitors!' Half dressed, I run to open the door a little and peer around. A footman dressed in full 18th-century livery holds out a red velvet cushion with an envelope on top.

'Ladies.' He bows. 'I bring word from the prince.'

'Thank you, kind sir.' I don't know the correct way to address him and can't curtsy to a footman in just my underwear. I smile sweetly, take the envelope, and thank him again, closing the door slowly.

Lexi and I both run and jump onto my bed, squealing.

'Lexi, it's addressed to you.'

I watch impatiently as she carefully peels open the gold wax seal stamped with *PC* and opens the envelope. She takes out a piece of blue-and-gold card and runs off to her bed to read it. Infuriating!

'Read it out loud!'

'But it was addressed to me.'

I grab a cushion and take aim.

'Ugh, fine.' She sighs. 'It's only an invitation from Prince Charming. He requests our presence in the Stage Garden at 8 o'clock.' She jumps up and down on her bed, whooping.

I find my phone to check the time. 'That's in eleven minutes!'

I drag Lexi into the bathroom to get washed while simultaneously tearing through our suitcases in search of toothbrushes and clean sets of clothes. I get a two-second shower, barely having enough time to rinse off my shampoo before we have to run.

* * *

At one minute to eight, we get to the elevator. As I twist my wet hair into a messy bun, Lexi giggles at my frazzled state, making me smile despite my racing heart. I savour the brief moment to catch my breath. That burst of activity was a bit much after a lazy day sitting on the bus.

We race on from the lobby, following the signposts to the Stage Garden – a vast lawn dotted with lanterns, with a gigantic open dome stage at the far end. Multi-coloured stage lights flash to upbeat music, pumping up the crowd for the show. Friendly staff in fairy costumes greet us at the garden entrance with big cups of tomato soup topped with heart-shaped croutons, then show us to our seats.

The plush sofas at the front of the seating area are all occupied by the most organised and speedy guests. All the late-coming families have their own snug area in a semi-circle at the back, with blankets and large floor cushions that are generously sprinkled with candy – much to Lexi's delight. And there's a mysterious hamper with a sign saying, *No peeking!*

Our cosy area to the side has a perfect view of the stage. We sink onto cushions so soft it feels as if we're levitating, and sip our delicious soup. 'I could get used to this life of luxury!' I tease, stretching out and stifling a yawn of contentment.

'Quick, Mum, it's starting!'

A portly older gentleman ambles on stage. With a booming American twang, he identifies himself as Mr Todgers, the resort owner, and welcomes his honoured guests, spreading his arms wide with a flourish.

I cough away a chuckle at his unfortunate name. Lexi looks at me curiously.

'What?'

I whisper in her ear, 'A todger is a man's willy!' She half-giggles and half looks... shocked I even know such words, surprised I find it amusing, and disappointed, as if her mother should grow up. What's wrong with children these days? Todger is funny!

Thankfully, the show then erupts into a dazzling display of colour and delight as our favourite fairy-tale characters fill the stage. There's Cinderella, in her gorgeous blue dress, Snow White, Little Red Riding Hood, and three little pigs, along with their menacing companion, the big bad wolf. They sing and dance against backdrops of daring acrobats and fire eaters, with explosions of colourful confetti. We cheer and laugh at their playful antics, and I feel a warm glow of joy as I watch Lexi singing along. Her eyes shine, caught up in the magic of her childhood storybooks bursting into life.

I'm in awe and decide in my next life, I'm coming back as a super-talented performer so I can be one of their gang.

When the show calls for volunteers, the children fall over themselves to be picked to take part on stage, and parents are up on their feet dancing and clapping. Despite Lexi's complaints, I am proud to be one of the loudest and most active parents joining in the fun.

But the revelry has only just begun. Next is the Fairy-Tale Parade. We finally get to open our hampers – which are full to the brim with dressing-up goodies. We eagerly search through the contents until Lexi selects a star-tipped wand and a glittering tiara, while I find some oversized plastic sunglasses, a neon tutu, and then throw a flamingo feather boa around my neck. Although Lexi doesn't verbally protest my public display of silliness, the roll of her eyes says it all. But she loosens up and giggles when she sees everyone else's ridiculous ensembles.

We take some bells and whistles, and when the entertainment cast jump from the stage and file through the centre of the audience, we follow their lead and join the procession.

A stilt-walking clown with a huge drum bangs a beat we all dance along to. We can't help but laugh, with each of us wearing funny costumes and doing silly dances. It's wonderful to see all the guests put their inhibitions aside to join in the fun. Come to think of it, where have my self-conscious barriers gone? Did I forget to pack them? I've got so used to being reserved and biting my tongue to avoid any confrontation at home, but here – being a fun mum is… fun!

With loud cheering, tambourines shaking, and horns honking, we parade around the Stage Garden, under floral arches, through the trees, and shimmy under limbo sticks that get lower and lower as we go. We conga and skip and eventually come back around to our seats.

Lexi and I collapse on our cushions, out of breath and delighted to find trays of cool drinks laid out for us. Flushed from dancing, Lexi takes a long slurp of her fruity drink, popping sweets into her mouth with abandon. 'That was awesome! Best show ever!'

I wipe the sweat from my forehead.

'So much fun! Isn't it amazing when everyone's not glued to their phones?'

'I don't have my own phone.' Lexi glares. Ah, probably best not to provoke another *worst mum in the world* conversation for not giving in to her constant phone requests. But it is great to see everyone enjoying themselves and taking part instead of taking photos and videos – and watching the show with their eyes, not through a screen. It's refreshingly liberating, like stepping back into the 90s.

I sink back into the soft cushions and enjoy my fruity cocktail. Out of the corner of my eye, I spot Lexi discreetly taking my phone out of my bag and switching on the camera. I don't want to ruin the mood by rising to her defiance right now, and secretly, I would also love a few snapshots of the show. At that point, all the lights go out. Dramatic music fills the darkness and laser beams flash through the sky. Then silence.

Brilliant lights flood the stage and a fanfare of trumpets blares out, signalling the highly anticipated arrival of the host of the evening, Prince Charming.

The crowd erupts in excited cheers as we all eagerly await his grand entrance. A burst of pyrotechnics suddenly explodes on stage, and I whoop as through the smoke, Prince Charming dramatically descends from the ceiling.

As he reaches the stage, he twirls into a dance, theatrically bowing and waving to the thrilled audience. Laughter, cheers, and music fill the air in a symphony of sound. But my mouth hangs open, unable to make a sound. I can't take my eyes off the man on stage.

Beneath a warm, golden spotlight, Prince Charming stands tall and confident, commanding attention as he welcomes the guests to the holiday resort. He's like no other man I have ever laid my eyes on. I am completely entranced.

My heart races as Prince Charming begins his speech. His warm and relaxed face captivates me, and I am mesmerised by the way his eyes sparkle as he flashes intoxicating smiles that show off his cute dimples and straight white teeth. I have never been this taken before, not even with the man I married. There's just no comparison.

My mind is in a whirlwind, and I have to check I'm not drooling. I take in his athletic build and broad shoulders and, eagerly pronounced in his princely tights, sculpted leg muscles and crown jewels on top of short, black hair that I want to run my fingers through.

I lean in closer, wanting to soak up every sound that comes out of his mouth. His voice has a fascinating tone that makes me feel something deep inside, a sensation I can't quite put my finger on.

I am in my own little world, barely taking in a word he says. All I know is that I need to know that man!

When he climbs onto the back of his large white horse, the rapturous applause brings me back down to earth.

'Lexi, what's happening? Is it finished?'

'No, he just said… he's searching for his one true love, and he asked if it could be anyone here.' She sounds exasperated. He rides through the seating, searching through the audience.

Women and girls are waving to catch his attention. As he comes closer to where we're sitting, my heart is going berserk. I'm so high on adrenaline that before I know it, I'm up on my feet, jumping, waving my arms in the air, shouting, 'Me! It's me! Over here!' As he trots past, he glances over and looks like he's stifling an out-of-character laugh. We only make eye contact for a split second, but my insides are doing somersaults.

When he's out of sight, I flop down and look at Lexi excitedly. I am met by a silent, epic glare.

When the show ends, I remember to take off my fancy dress, and float back to our room with Lexi following behind. I perch on the bed, my heart still racing. What was that? I have never experienced such instant, overwhelming attraction. We've been in Fairy-Tale Wonderland for two minutes, and I've already fallen in love at first sight. I giggle at how ridiculous that sounds.

Photos! Did Lexi get a picture of him? Scrambling to get my phone out of my bag, my hands fumble to scroll through the few photos Lexi took… There! I zoom in as much as the camera allows – I didn't imagine it! He really is dreamy! I fall back on my bed with a sigh.

Lexi runs into the room and dramatically faints on her bed.

'Mum, I'm in love.' She sighs.

'Me too.' I sigh as well.

'Huh?' She props herself up on her elbow to look at me quizzically.

'Hmm? Oh, I asked, *with who*?'

'Jack!' She swoons, placing the back of her hand against her forehead.

I stare, then giggle. 'Wait, Jack from Jack and the Beanstalk?'

'Yes, Mum. Don't laugh; I'm serious.' She stares up at the ceiling and lets out a deep, dramatic sigh. A smile tugs at my lips.

We both lie dreaming of pretty boys.

Boys! I snort to myself. I am probably old enough to be Prince Charming's mother. That thought wipes the smile clean off my face. I am certainly old enough to know better, that's for sure.

Stay Calm, Be Cool

How are people supposed to get up on time without a dog licking their nose, wanting his breakfast? I miss my little Barney dog. It's infuriating that I couldn't trust Ben to keep him alive for a few days while we're away. Although I'm sure he's having fun at his boarding kennel doggy hotel. But now, according to Princess Bear, Lexi and I have precisely eight minutes to be up and out of the door, ready for the morning's first scheduled activity.

'I'm going for a funky fairy-tale vibe today.' I fling on my jeans, *rock-chick princess* t-shirt, and my favourite silver sequined Converse. 'What do you reckon?'

Dressed all in pink and looking cute hugging her Princess Bear tightly, Lexi rolls her eyes. I playfully squeeze her cheeks. 'Come on, my little cupcake. Let's hope we haven't missed breakfast.'

Lexi skips ahead towards the staircase at the end of the gold-muralled corridor, keen to discover the fun today will bring. I need coffee. I'm not sure I can cope with anything parade-like this early in the morning.

Lexi sashays down the sweeping staircase. 'Look, Mum, I'm a movie star!' She turns back to me with mischief in her eyes. 'Am I allowed to slide down the bannister?'

'No!' Although, it is tempting to swing a leg over and whizz down.

At the foot of the stairs, a weathered wooden signpost points the way to adventure – left to Fairies, right to Dragons.

'Which do you fancy, Lex?'

'I'm going to choose... fairies.' Lexi skips through the door to the left and we follow a trail of rose petals down the steps outside. This is our first view of the gardens in daylight. Their website wasn't exaggerating about the sprawling emerald lawns and kaleidoscope of florals. The petals lead us past a massive tree of lights on the village green and along one of the many meandering paths bordered by the stunning displays of colourful blooms. It's like we are in nature's very own fairy garden.

The petal trail takes us through a fragrant rose garden and under a tunnel of pink rose arches. Lexi hops along the stepping stones, and we come to a wonderful garden where the fairy staff and children are gathered.

As we pass, a shower of rainbow glitter flutters from the trees, causing Lexi to gasp in amazement. 'Did you see that? Real fairy dust!' she exclaims, jumping up with her hands outstretched to catch the glitter drifting down. 'This is the best day ever!'

Lexi's eyes widen as she takes in the details of our surroundings. 'Look, Mum! Fairy doors!' She points to the trees outlining the lawn. At their roots are bright little doors – some are surrounded by miniature gardens with tiny tables and chairs, and I even spot some teeny fairy dresses pegged to a mini washing line. We walk through an inner circle of lavender plants swarming with real butterflies and bees, and discover gorgeous little fairy houses scattered throughout. If I was only a few feet shorter, I'd be packing my bags and moving straight in.

'Look, Mum! That cottage looks like it's made of chocolate!' Lexi jumps down on her hands and knees to take a closer look. 'I wonder if we're allowed to lick it?'

'No!' I laugh, not quite sure if she is serious or not.

We aim towards the centre of the enchanting garden, where children gather around red toadstool tables to collect their fairy costumes. I would have loved this when I was a little girl. It's a shame I can't stay and play. But I have to work; that's why we're here after all. A young girl in a pinafore runs towards Lexi with a broad smile. 'Come and get your costume!'

Without hesitation, Lexi takes the girl's hand. 'See you later, Mum.' I plant a kiss on her cheek, ignoring the look on her face as she rubs it off, and leave for my meeting.

When I take a quick glance back, I'm pleased to see Lexi laughing with a group of girls. Hopefully this kids' club will help her find her confidence again. I'm relieved she has managed to fit straight in and isn't the shy, quiet girl in the corner like I used to be.

Heading back through the bounty of roses, I spot a team of ninja-like caterers stealthily setting up breakfast for the fairy children. In just seconds, the team erects a table and begins staging it to fairy perfection. More ninjas swiftly arrive with trays and teapots and trolleys of cake stands. It's an impressive, efficient operation to make things magically appear.

Although I feel jittery about making a good impression when I meet the bosses at the welcome meeting, there's a calming atmosphere in the resort. Starting the day with the sun on my face and a stroll through such beautiful gardens is a world away from the usual morning rush to get Lexi to school. The familiar sounds of city traffic and construction work fade into memory, replaced by cheery birdsong. I feel strangely light and airy. I'm even swinging my arms as I walk towards the meeting, breathing in the sweet, fresh air.

Perhaps I could get a job here as a cleaner or a waitress? My heart rate quickens at the thought of waking up here every morning. But it slows again as I remember how much I hate cleaning. And with my butterfingers, I'd get sacked on my first day. How disappointing. That was a very short-lived 21st-century Shirley Valentine fantasy.

Then I catch sight of dreamy Prince Charming striding past the massive tree in front of me. *Stay calm, be cool.* My body doesn't listen. My face flushes, and all those butterflies now seem to be fluttering in my stomach. He glances around, and our eyes fleetingly meet. My heart rate goes into overdrive. What is wrong with me? This is not a normal reaction. He's heading towards the meeting hall. My breath catches sharply in my throat as I realise I might actually get to meet this handsome leading cast member in just a few moments.

I can almost hear my mother's nagging voice telling me I shouldn't be looking at other men when I'm a married woman. But it doesn't do any harm to admire someone from afar and maybe play out a fantasy or two in my mind. Surely my mind is the one place I get to keep all to myself? Surely I don't have to put Ben first in my fantasies too?

It's not as if Prince Heartthrob would look twice at a middle-aged, frumpy mum. Even my own husband doesn't notice me. I take a deep breath, scrunch up my curls, and speed walk after him to the meeting.

***

As I enter the hall, my shoulders immediately hunch and I want to merge into the background. Straight ahead, the staff chat in their small groups, dressed impeccably in their smart uniforms. Guests mill to the right, all in couples and dressed in their Sunday best. Then there's me – all by myself and dressed as a *funky rock-chick princess,* which is not quite the appropriate attire. I shuffle over to the left, next to the breakfast buffet, and make a beeline for the coffee.

But this is no ordinary English breakfast buffet. It is a visual feast of mouth-watering delicacies that makes my stomach rumble – a bit different to my usual daytime diet of caffeine and anxiety.

Coffee in hand, I squeal inwardly as I scan the delicious-looking goodies. Everything on the long wooden table is dainty and bite-size: mini Danish pastries, croissants, cinnamon rolls. I take one of each to try. I pick up the cutest hard-boiled egg decorated like a unicorn head, marvelling at the minute eyelashes made of tiny flecks of dill that must have been placed by the tiniest, steadiest hands. Elves, no doubt. Then a tiny gingerbread man-shaped pancake and a heart-shaped pancake with choco-late sauce and raspberry coulis both join the party on my plate. And for balance, I place a large handful of berries precariously on top of the pile, and edge to the side of the table.

I recognise the loud voice of Mr Todgers, the resort manager, and look up to see him mingling with the guests on the other side of the large hall. I watch him working the room while I pop berries in my mouth. He makes the women laugh politely and shakes hands with the men. He's elegantly dressed in a deep-purple velvet jacket and oozes money and charm.

The hall begins to fill, and a young woman in a navy trouser suit and sensible shoes squeezes beside me. She seems totally unaware that she's invading my personal space and almost standing on my feet. She squashes me against the table, standing stiffly upright, holding a tea-cup and saucer. I'm trapped and feel like a short, awk-ward teenager next to her.

Then *he* appears across the room and my heart rate shoots up to what must be a dangerous level. Out of cos-tume today, he looks suave and professional in a sharp black suit and waistcoat, crisp white shirt, and silver tie. His hair is shiny and slicked back from his handsome face. He chats warmly with some of the maintenance staff and heads over to the guests. I watch the women become magnetised by his charisma. They seem to drift towards him – all vying for his attention, which he happily gives with a knockout smile and those damn cute dimples of his. Oh my gosh! What if I got to interview him? And got one of those delicious smiles to be directed at me? Purely for professional purposes, obviously.

Oh shitake! He's coming this way! My heart is in my mouth, and I'm seconds away from needing a paper bag to hyperventilate into. My cheeks flush, and I don't know what to do with myself. I dip my head so I don't stare, but he's coming straight towards me. My breathing is fast and heavy, and my jaw clenches. I sneak a peek for a split second, long enough to see how utterly gorgeous he is up close and see that he has stopped right in front of me. I gulp and stop breathing. He's right there. He leans in and reaches a hand behind me to take an apple from the table. I look up and give a tight smile, but he is looking at my generously heaped plate, and his eyebrow raises – just a tiny bit. I get flustered and panic and clear my plate slightly by shoving a pancake in my mouth with my fingers.

At the moment I realise I don't have a napkin, Mr Todgers puts an arm around Prince Charming's shoulder and manoeuvres him to face me.

'I see you're making good use of our all-inclusive facilities.' Mr Todgers snorts. He waves his hand towards Miss Navy Suit beside me. 'This is Julie Tattley, a reporter for the broadsheets.' He shakes her hand and then holds out his hand to me.

'You must be the other reporter, Cathy Jackson.'

Mouth too full to speak, I blink hard and shake his hand. With chocolate sauce and raspberry coulis-covered fingers.

If he's noticed, he doesn't react. My eyes fly to Prince Charming. He's staring at the mess I've left on Mr Todgers' hand. My stomach lurches.

'Cahhy,' I correct him, covering my overstuffed mouth with my breakfast-splattered hand.

Mr Todgers looks at me, raising his eyebrows. Eyes still on me, he slowly gestures with his mucky hand. 'Have you met our Prince Charming and head of entertainment, joining us all the way from Korea?'

Prince Charming gives a slight nod with a stern facial expression like he's about to scold us.

'Could I arrange a time for an interview?' Miss Suit asks Prince Charming. He looks over her head and out of the windows at the side of the room.

'No, sorry. I'm too busy.'

'Pleasure to meet you both. Excuse us.' Mr Todgers ushers Prince Charming away.

I finally get to chew and swallow. Well, that did not go well. I lick my fingers. My chest is tense. I try to process what just happened, making rapid side glances, avoiding the awkward silence with Miss Suit. Brushing over the chocolate debacle, was I just snubbed? Where was my smile? What did I do? I pull my lips back in from their pout. I need a second chance to make a good first impression. And I need him to agree to an interview with me.

I look up to see Prince Charming about to walk past towards the door. I toss my plate on the table, barge my way free from my squashed position, and step forward, raising my hand like a school kid.

'Sorry, excuse me, Prince Charming...'

He turns towards me and his face drops. His unfriendly reaction makes my mind go completely blank. I have to speak *right now* before he passes.

'Erm, do you... like... cheese?'

My eyes ping open wide and I gasp, as shocked as everyone else at the words that just fell out of my mouth. I hear a snort from Miss Suit behind me. Without a flicker on Prince Charming's face or a break in his stride, he snaps, 'No.'

I freeze. My mind screams.

'Man of few words, I see,' I mutter, I guess to Miss Suit. 'I'm just going to get some air.'

I flee out of the door in the corner of the room and head to an exit. The door's signed *Private*, but a private space to hide is just what I need. I head outside and slump back against the door, breathing like I've just run a marathon.

Do. You. Like. Cheese.

What the...? I slap my forehead and hold my head in my palm. I've royally screwed up this time. Taking a few deep breaths, I reach into my over-the-shoulder bag for the sneaky pack of cigarettes I carry for times like this – when I'm relieved to still be an occasional social smoker. Well, a social-anxiety smoker, if I'm being honest. I hate to imagine Ben's reaction if he knew. I light up and take a long drag. I bet Prince Charming can't wait for an interview after that scintillating first question. But anyway, who doesn't like cheese?

I lift my head to scan my surroundings and check I haven't stumbled into something *too* private. It's all quiet, so I walk down the short path leading to a small courtyard – a quaint, dark, cobbled paving area hidden between the building walls. Hopefully all this greenery will help me calm. Ivy covers the walls, and huge potted ferns surround tree trunk tables. It's beautifully staged with thick white candles and strings of round white bulbs trailing above, and exactly the kind of peaceful garden I would love to have at home.

As I lean against the wall, a noise catches my attention. I scrunch my eyes to see behind the metal table and chairs with meticulously placed cushions. I make out a head of black hair... a figure crouching, talking into a phone. My heart stops beating. I quickly look away. Of course, it would be him. My blood pressure must be sky high.

What on earth can I say so he doesn't think I'm a lunatic?

I've got nothing.

Halfway through my cigarette, he stands and walks in my direction. I watch him, waiting for eye contact so I can smile and say something sensible that I haven't yet thought of. He looks straight ahead, stony-faced, talking on the phone in, I presume, Korean. He's just about to pass, and I take a deep breath. Come on, brain, think! He turns his head as he approaches. 'You have...' He gestures with a finger from his chin to his chest. I look down and he's gone.

I drag my hand down my face and blow out the breath I've been holding in. I squidge out the cigarette and then search for a scrap of tissue at the bottom of my bag to wipe off the chocolate that has dripped all down my t-shirt. I pull out a compact mirror and open it to find chocolate smudged over my chin. I'm never eating chocolate again.

I slowly return inside to the meeting room, now chock-a-block with staff and more guests. I'm late, as usual. Mr Todgers is finishing his introductory pleasantries as I squeeze my way through to my standing point next to Miss Suit.

'I'd like to introduce you all to two reporters who are watching us this week – Julie Tattley and Cathy Jackson.' I give a tight-lipped smile in response, but then can't hold back a giant, mischievous grin when I spot the chocolate smear across Mr Todgers' cheek.

'Remember, we make *all* our guests feel like VIPs, even reporters digging around for dirt.' Mr Not-Funny-Todgers chortles to himself and looks towards the staff. 'Make sure you keep your gossip on the DL.'

A few feet shuffle. Once he pauses for breath, I call aloud, 'Cally.'

Mr Not-Funny-Todgers looks round at me indifferently, as though I have just blurted out a random word.

'My name's Cally, not Cathy.' I smile sweetly as all faces turn towards me. He ignores my outburst and continues speaking.

I will myself to fade back into the wall, avoiding all eye contact and pitying glances. 'If everyone could stop looking at me now, that would be great,' I mumble to myself.

That's more than enough embarrassment for one morning. I skulk backwards out of the meeting, feeling like I'm sliding down a long snake away from my promotion, back to square one.

* * *

Ahhh, now this is the life. I sink into the warm bubbles, aches and embarrassment rippling away. Soaking in a jacuzzi to begin a luxurious adults' spa day while the children are entertained at the kids' club – what more could a mama want? Ooh, champagne! Don't mind if I do. The smart poolside barman hands me a glass. The alcohol goes down rather too well, and as it fizzes up my nose, I realise it is only 10.30 am. Oh well, I'm on holiday. I mean, working holiday. This counts as work, right? Maybe I'll have a swim and then a massage. I need to try the full spa experience to write about it later.

Time to relax. I wonder if I can remember how. It's been a long while. I lean back and gaze up at the domed ceiling with its ornate tiles around the rim, dimly lit in orange. I think I'm supposed to close my eyes, clear my mind, and take deep breaths – in through the nose, out through the mouth.

In... I check my bikini top is covering everything it should.

Out... What a treat!

In... This is much better than a stupid meeting.

Out... Stupid chocolate.

In... What if I can't get an interview with Prince Charming?

Out... What if my review is rubbish and Mr Todgers charges me for our stay?

In... What if I end up getting the sack?

I sit up in a panic. This isn't relaxing at all. How am I supposed to stop thinking and fidgeting? There's so much to explore; I can't just sit here doing nothing but worry.

I take in my lavish surroundings – gold-veined creamy marble and soft up lighting. It's all very minimal and grown up, in stark contrast to the riot of colour throughout the rest of the resort. Palm trees outline the long turquoise pool in the centre of the spa, the bar at

one side, my jacuzzi at the far end. Vines of white roses climb around marble columns, and panpipe melodies
and the scent of jasmine float through the air – the spa
would be a tranquil haven were it not for the incessant
nattering coming from across the pool.

I close my eyes again and try to block out the young
yummy mummies' chattering. Perhaps the type of person
who can afford to come here doesn't need to unwind as
desperately as me. Maybe they're more used to visiting
spas – leaving their babies with nannies while they're pampered and preened. Though, none of these women look
like they've recently had a baby; they each look toned,
tanned, and groomed. My inner green-eyed monster rears
its ugly head. I look down and prod my well-rounded,
long-standing *mummy pouch*, thankful for the cover of
water. What on earth possessed me to wear a bikini for
the first time in over a decade?

'We need more bubbles!' shrills a voice from above.
My eyes fly up to see Mrs Life-and-Soul-of-the-Party
pouring pink goop into the water. Before my heart has
time to sink, she shrieks with laughter and takes off
her robe, ready to join my *relaxing* jacuzzi. The water
whirls, turning goop into bubbles. The heap of bubbles
expands rapidly, soon becoming an avalanching mountain of foam. The water jets activate again, sweeping
me into the centre of the bubbly pool, and I slip under
the water.

My feet slide on the tiles, and I grapple for enough
anchorage to thrust myself back up. But I'm pulled further under and swallow mouthfuls of rose-flavoured
bubbles. At last, when I manage to get a toe-grip on the
skiddy floor for a second, I splash my way up to gasp

for air. Mrs Life-and-Soul is waving her arms, her head whipping around. I catch one of the words she screams: '*drowning*'.

I can't keep my head above water. Arms flailing, feet still slipping, my strength dwindles, and my lungs burn.

Just as I conclude this is it, the end – death by bubbles – my arm is grabbed.

I emerge from Bubble Mountain, gasping and spluttering. My rescuer reaches out and wraps his arms around me, pulling me out of Foam Hell to safety. I cling to him like a limpet, my body weak and exhausted, my mind disoriented. Even Mrs Life-and-Soul seems to be shocked into silence.

It's only when he wraps a fluffy towel around me that I recognise my life-saving hero. I have literally just been saved by Prince Charming.

I wipe away the foam-covered hair splodged over my face. And I'm facing his smooth, muscular, bare chest.

My eyes are drawn up to his face, and I gasp. I try to thank him, but the words won't come out. All I can do is stare. I am lost in his beautiful dark eyes and mesmerised by the flawless golden skin that highlights his masculine bone structure – high cheekbones and strong, square jawline.

I don't have mere butterflies in my stomach; I have huge fireworks exploding right now.

Prince Charming pats my back. 'Are you all right?' His eyes are fraught with concern. I nod, still trying to catch my breath.

I cough and look down. Big mistake. Now my eyes have wandered down to his impressive abs. My cheeks are burning, and I blink rapidly, not sure where to avert my eyes. My heart is pounding and I feel quite light-headed, but I manage to breathe out, 'I'm fine. Thank you for saving me.'

He puts his arm around my shoulders and lowers his head to make eye contact.

'Can I help you to a seat? Do you need a glass of water?' Although he looks anxious, he sounds confident and in control. My gaze is transfixed on his lips. They're so full and kissable.

Up this close, he is breathtaking, and his attention makes me tingle all over. I smooth down my hair and try to hide how fast I'm breathing.

'Honestly, I'm OK, thank you.' I cover a cough with my hand.

'Can I get someone for you? Your husband perhaps?'

'I'm just here with my daughter. I'll go and get changed. I'll be fine. Thank you again, you're very kind.'

Oh no, now I'm wittering.

'That must have been a terrible shock. I want to see that you're OK.'

I dip my head, squinting. 'I'm fine now. Just a bit embarrassed for being an idiot.'

He still has his arm around me and squeezes my shoulder.

'Not at all. It was an accident. I'm glad I was close enough to help you.'

I look up into my hero's kind face. I don't mean to look at him adoringly, but I can't tear my eyes away.

'Thank you.' I give a shy smile as his eyes scan me all over, making sure I am OK.

'You're very welcome.' His face warms. He's not at all like the impolite and unfriendly man I met earlier. Perhaps he doesn't recognise me in this half-drowned state. I would love to stay here, soaking up his attention, but I'm keen for this whole embarrassing fiasco to be over. And this overwhelming desire for him to ease up.

The barman comes to my side to check on me, and while I am vaguely aware of his profuse apologies, my focus is firmly centred on Prince Eye-Candy-Baywatch-Babe walking back to the side of the pool. I have to fan my glowing face with my hand. Prince Charming, about to dive, wearing nothing but tiny trunks.

With as much poise as I can muster, I put on my complimentary soft white slippers and, with my dripping head held high, flip-flop my way towards the changing rooms. As I pass the pool, my gaze lingers on my hero expertly diving and then gliding underwater with graceful dolphin kicks like a beautiful merman before his arms sweep powerfully through the water.

Prince Charming is a handsome, muscular, Korean water god. A glistening, Golden Adonis. The man of the dreams I didn't even know I had. Or my new wet-and-wild fantasy, anyway.

Well, this hasn't been the most relaxing spa visit, and now I need a cold shower to calm the lust I didn't know I was capable of feeling.

On the plus side, I don't think anyone noticed my belly.

TUESDAY

Annyeonghaseyo

Got it! An idea strikes as I walk to the dining hall. I'll speak to him in Korean! Maybe that will get Prince Charming's attention in a more positive way. Although an interview seems unlikely at the moment, surely it will get me a smile, at least?

I have a few minutes to spare before the fairy children are ready for lunch. It's a toss-up: change my chocolatey t-shirt or learn Korean? Korean it is. I hide behind a tree and sneak out my phone, feeling like a naughty little girl.

How do I say hello in Korean?

안녕하세요
annyeonghaseyo

Erm... Perhaps I should have gone to get changed.

I listen to the translator and repeat '*An-nyong-ha-say-oh*' over and over. Easy peasy. I hide my phone in my bag and creep back out, giving my shoulders a smug little wiggle at my brainwave. Now to wait for the right moment...

I hear the rumble of stampeding fairies before they come into sight. An excited horde of smiling faces, flower crowns, and wings comes running towards me. A small, familiar hand grabs my arm amid the rush, pulling me in the direction of the lunchtime feeding frenzy. The crowd slows as fairies find their parents and form a queue to enter the dining hall. I was always under the impression that fairies were quiet and shy, but this lot all chatter non-stop. Loudly. I haven't understood a word from my gabbling child fairy, but I get the distinct impression she has enjoyed her morning.

Lexi falls silent when it's our turn to enter the building, briefly overwhelmed by the Enchanted Forest enticing us inside. The banquet hall is lit in violet, with a canopy of purple wisteria hanging from the ceiling. Long tables are interspersed with leafy trees sparkling with little lanterns. We find seats next to Lexi's new friends and their families. It feels like we're guests at a classy wedding reception; I can't believe we're being treated like all the people who have paid to be here.

The table centrepieces are lifted straight from a woodland fantasy photoshoot – moss table runners with thick log slices, fragrant floral displays, and strings of fairy lights. So much imaginative attention to detail has gone into this lunch – I can barely cope with organising a simple birthday party for eight kids! At her last birthday,

I only just remembered to get Lexi a birthday cake, and even then, I forgot to buy candles.

Children watch with starry eyes as the fairy servers set down glasses of slushed ice lemonade, which magically changes from a deep purple colour to pink.

'All natural, no artificial colours in the drinks or food.' Our server beams as she brings the grown-ups drinks with ice cubes that have tiny edible flowers frozen inside. With each sip of pink liquor, a burst of strawberries and cream dances on my tongue, giddiness rising in me like bubbles.

Against a background of noisy slushie slurping, we browse the menus laid at our place settings.

Unicorn Summer Rolls with Unicorn Dip

Unicorn Noodles

Unicorn Sundae

Eat me!

I am the first to take a bite of the intriguing menu. It's tasteless, but the look on the nearby children's faces is priceless. Lexi looks utterly horrified and almost hides under the table. 'Mmm, it's pretty good. Try it!' Lexi's friend bravely nibbles a corner. It's too hilarious not to take another bite before I come clean. 'It's rice paper, and these are edible flowers.' I laugh. Lexi sits up and giggles, but she can't be persuaded to even give it a lick. I'm relieved my hunch was correct; otherwise I don't think she would have spoken to me again.

When our starters arrive, the children enthuse about their morning's magical fairy trail and dragon hunt while tucking into a rainbow of vegetables. Although the healthy goodness is hidden in plain sight, including ingredients that Lexi would never usually touch, her plate is soon empty.

But it's our *unicorn noodles* that deserve pride of place on Instagram. As the fairies squeeze wedges of lemon over the top, the noodles change from deep purple to lilac to pink, and the hall fills with awestruck gasps and wows. Lexi's fingers dance with her fork as she playfully twirls the noodles. 'Mum, can you make this when we're back home?'

'Um, I don't think they sell this at the supermarket,' I jest. 'But maybe, if we can find a magic spell book!'

Mealtimes are forever ruined. Nothing will ever live up to this dining experience. Particularly with my culinary skills.

As we tuck in, Prince Charming nears our table, dressed in full fairy-tale prince regalia. He is staring directly at me. Does he recognise me as the drowning idiot he had to rescue? Although, he's staring directly at my chest, to be precise. I'm immediately hot and flustered, and not just because of the image of those tiny trunks that comes to mind. But then I squirm in my seat; he must have noticed I still have chocolate smudged on my t-shirt.

'Mum, people keep staring at your rock princess t-shirt,' Lexi whispers behind her hand. 'I think you should change.'

'Why? What's wrong with it?' I snort, sneaking a glance at the back of my hero.

She shakes her head. 'I just can't.'

'Can't what?' Oof. Kids can be so mean! This tween age is tough, but if I want to raise a strong, independent young woman, I guess I have to put up with a bit of sass along the way. I poke my fingers into her ribs, making her giggle but also accidentally fling pink noodles off her fork.

'Surely there are some cool princesses too?' I gather the noodles blighting the flower display across the table. 'They can't all like needlepoint and spinning wheels?'

'Mum, stop saying *cool*. No one says that anymore.' She whispers the word *cool* in case anyone should hear.

'You should be thankful you've got such a cool, hip, and trendy mum. Not everyone's as lucky as you!' I tease.

She puts her head in her hands. 'So. Embarrassing.' But she can't hide the smile in her voice.

Our *unicorn sundaes* arrive looking like a candy shop exploded in a glass. I would usually gain extra inches just by looking at all that cream, but it could be magically calorie-free and I think I deserve a treat today. 'Oh Lex, I meant to ask, do you know what *on the DL* means?'

'On the down-low.' Her eyes roll a full 360 degrees. I look at her blankly.

'It means keeping quiet. But you were born in the 1900s, you're way too old to use words like that.'

Ouch! Now I feel so... past my use-by date.

The meal finishes with a strong, morale-boosting Irish coffee. Although, I'm not used to day-drinking, and my body's not sure if it wants to party or fall asleep in a corner.

***

After lunch, guests and staff congregate on the lush carpet of perfectly groomed lawn on the village green. Children huddle around each member of the fairy-tale cast – hands in the air, all talking at once and tapping for attention. The poor staff inside those furry bear and wolf suits must be sweltering. It makes me go right off the idea of joining the entertainer gang, with kids jumping around your feet all day. And yet each character remains calm and smiley (those whose faces aren't hidden by large mascot heads, anyway). I'm impressed by their patience (and heat tolerance).

Everyone looks so carefree and happy enjoying a sunny afternoon. There is an energy of fun and adventure with nowhere urgent to be and nothing that can't wait until tomorrow.

Lexi joins the ring around three bears, and I make myself comfortable under the shade of the massive tree. A small brass plaque on my bench says *Tree of Dreams*. How lovely! I look down at my hand. Oops! I seem to have brought another glass of the pink drink with me. I could get used to this kind of working day.

My eyes keep being drawn to Prince Charming. Actually, he's pretty much the only person I'm watching. He definitely has a *sexiest dad in the playground* thing going on. It's not just that, though; I love the way he holds the children's hands and crouches and leans in, taking an interest in what they say to him. I can see they all adore him. And he looks like he's genuinely having fun with them. The way he has a toddler sitting on his shoulders who's holding on to his ears makes me love him even more. Love? I've barely spoken to the man! How strong are these drinks?

Now the games have begun, it's hard to catch a glimpse of Lexi amongst the playful pandemonium. But then I see her – hula hooping with the three bears. I love how she's engaging with the activities without having to act *cool* in front of her school friends.

The look on her face reminds me of how happy she was playing with Ben when she was younger. It must really hurt that he never makes time to play with her these days. I used to see how special it made her feel when he took her to the park, before he was always too busy and work became his priority. And now when he's home, his computer and *I've just got to take this outside* phone calls are more important than family time. This realisation makes my heart ache. I've been too busy managing our lives to stop and properly notice before. My poor baby.

The fairy crew from lunch draw my attention as they run past to join the others. After a couple of minutes, a wave of excitement ripples through the crowd of children and they run off in all directions. Lexi runs past, throwing her teddy bear at me to look after and yelling that they're searching for a key to the big treasure chest the fairies have found. I am content relaxing under the Tree of Dreams, wondering what a group of fairies might be called. A flock of fairies, perhaps? Or maybe a flutter of fairies?

A woman with a big, high-tech camera suddenly appears through a gap in the plants to my side, making my eyes fly open wide and my body stiffen. I try to recollect what was said about photographers in the resort. Action shots, photo books. I'm not sure about being spied on. I hate having my photo taken at the best of times. Although I'm happy I don't feel a need to live up to impossible *hot girl summer* beauty standards and can embrace my *feral* authenticity, that doesn't necessarily mean I want my chocolate-smudged t-shirt caught on camera. I dip my head to make myself invisible as she passes.

Noticing Lexi's bear next to me on the bench, I pick her up. 'What do you have to say today, Princess Bear?' I press her paw.

'It's a great day to play and have fun!' Her cute electronic voice is drowned out by a young boy yelling. He runs across the green holding out a large key, and the children make their way towards the treasure chest. I finish my drink and stand up – the bear says it's time for fun mum to party – I mean, play. Who am I to argue?

The atmosphere is electric as the children wait to discover the surprise inside the huge wooden chest. The fairies fuel the anticipation and excitement until the children are ready to burst. Even Miss Suit has come to see what's in the box. The boy who found the key is rewarded with the honour of opening the chest...

We count down from three, he twists the key, the fairies lift the lid, and confetti bombs explode, delighting the children with flower petals fluttering down over them. The chest is full to the brim with fairy-tale fancy-dress costumes.

Children bundle forward and, one by one, transform into princesses and knights, dragons and jesters, wizards and mermaids. I catch a fleeting glimpse of a very happy Lexi with a bear costume while I wait for a turn.

I cross my fingers as I lean over the chest, hoping for an adult-sized Cinderella dress. A fairy hands me a unicorn costume – a white cloak with a rainbow tail, and a headdress with a golden horn and rainbow mane. It's cute, and I can be a unicorn this time. I spot Miss Suit peering into the chest.

'Which costume are you going to choose?' I ask with a smirk, pointing to a dragon costume. She straightens up as if embarrassed to be caught looking.

'None. I have work to do.' She gives me a stern glare and marches off. That told me! I know I have work to do too, but this is research! I can worry about the writing part later. I wonder if Miss Suit ever lets herself have fun.

'Hide and seek! We'll give you to the count of twenty to hide!' shouts the fairy leader. I am now a slightly tipsy unicorn. With my horn wobbling as I run to find a hiding place, I take a random path and squeeze my way through a bush to hide. I'm out of breath, not sure if it's from excitement or the exertion of running. I can't see anyone else from my spot, and I wait a good ten minutes before I poke my face through the leaves to have a peep.

With a twig in my ear and a leaf tickling my chin, I peek around and then draw my head back in as quickly as possible without piercing myself. Dressed as a fairy godmother, there's no mistaking the physique of Prince Charming searching in the opposite direction. My heart pounds wildly. I want him to see that I'm not just a choc-olate-dribbling airhead who drowns in bubbles.

I gently squeeze out through the bush. My mane gets tangled in the twigs, tugging my head backwards, and I fiddle quietly to free myself. Prince Charming still has his back turned. Possessed by mischief and pink liquor, I find the temptation too hard to resist. I mime creeping like a burglar along the path and sneak up behind him. Then, just as I'm about to pinch his bottom, my one remaining sensible brain cell screams at my hand, *Don't do it! It's sexual harassment in the workplace!* and I dive into the closest bush to hide.

What they don't show in the movies is that bushes do not make a soft landing, and twigs and leaves do not support a person's weight. *At all.* With loud cracking, rustling, and some snorting, I fall to the ground, legs v-shaped in the air, twigs poking in all kinds of places they shouldn't. And I'm stuck. *#FAIL.*

I'm breathing fast and trying not to roar with laughter when Prince Charming's face appears through the leaves. He stares at me for a moment, his eyebrow raised, and I detect a slight smirk. Not quite a smile, but it must be a step in the right direction.

'Onion-gassy-ho!' I pronounce in my very British accent. I wave with a big smile and awkwardly make a heart shape with my fingers. With just a hint of a grin, but smiling eyes, he shakes his head.

'You're going to be trouble, I can tell.'

Thankfully, he offers out his hands. As he pulls me up, leaves fall out of my hair, twigs fall from my shoulder, and he catches me in his arms as I fall into him in fits of giggles for three glorious seconds before the screams of nearing children end the moment.

I think now might be a good time for a sobering snooze.

***

Loud banging wakes me with a jump. It's pitch black, and I'm not sure where I am. I slowly come round. Hotel room. Knocking. Door. Now it makes sense. I heave myself upright and feel my way through the dark. I fumble to find the light switch and eventually open the door to a smiling Nanny P and a scowling Lexi.

'Hurry up – it's festival time! Come on.' Lexi yanks me out of the door, and I just manage to grab a hoodie before my arm is pulled from its socket. I hate to imagine the state I must look; I hide inside my hoodie and pull the hood down low. So, festival...

Please, no parades or bushes. Or cheese. Or bubbles.

The Stage Garden is an extravaganza of lights, colour, and music, with crowds of guests laughing and enjoying the festival. We follow a path lit by twinkling star-shaped lanterns creating a magical ambience as we weave through the stalls of fanciful food, games, and performances.

My dehydrated tongue is stuck to the roof of my mouth, and I grab a glass from the first silver-tray-holding barman we come to. Non-alcoholic liquid – bliss! Meanwhile, Lexi twirls around, the colourful lights sparkling in her eyes. 'Wow! This place is bomb!'

I think that means Lexi approves as she skips along, tempted to simultaneously join the guests dancing to the live band and toast marshmallows on the large campfire. Then she's captivated by the bees and butterflies with enormous wings passing by on stilts and wants to follow as they flutter through the crowds.

'How do you fancy practising your bow and arrow skills here?'

'Not yet.' She skips ahead and I grab her hand so I don't lose her.

'How about creating some art with these squirt guns filled with paints?'

'I want to see *everything* first.' She tugs my arm past marquees holding drumming workshops and kids learning circus skills.

We finally stop at the barbecue, where the food looks as delicious as it smells. We choose our burgers and eat while we continue our tour.

Towards the end of the festival trail in lands as yet unexplored, the atmosphere becomes more peaceful and children are listening to stories in a candlelit area with cosy rugs and cushions. A giant yurt is the final festival destination. We hover in the entranceway, giggling at an exuberant wizard hosting a potion-making workshop.

I hang my arm around Lexi's shoulder. 'Wow! How fun is this? What do you fancy trying?'

'I'm going to have my face painted and get some glitter tattoos.' Lexi skips off again to wait on a tree-stump stool. As I eye the lovely snuggly area, my body begs to rest; it's been a long day. As I go to sit down, I notice the storyteller has changed. Now Prince Charming is reading. My shattered body perks up instantly.

I tiptoe to the log next to Prince Charming and manage to sit without embarrassing myself. Win! I try to focus on the story instead of watching his beautiful lips, but his handsome face and lyrical voice has me hooked.

When the story finishes, the children all clap and disperse; then, just as I'm about to strike up a conversation, a face appears between us. Miss Suit, who seems... different. It takes a moment to register that she looks odd because she's grinning, but not in a happy way.

'Have you seen who's here?' She looks at us in turn and we both shake our heads.

Menacing. Her grin is menacing.

'Singer... girl group... have a guess. I'm going to get a photo.' Her eyes light up as she sneers, 'She's so drunk, she's falling around everywhere. It's hilarious.'

Neither Prince Charming nor I take the bait. He busies himself sorting a pile of storybooks, and I turn to check on Lexi.

'Don't you want to know?'

'No, thank you.' I frown. Not only has she interrupted my attempt to convince Prince Charming that I am actually professional and worthy of speaking to, but I don't like her manner. She's gone from snooty and uptight to sounding like tabloid trash out to cause trouble. The last thing someone needs when they embarrass themselves in public is photographic evidence. I should know!

Prince Charming doesn't even look up.

'Fine, looks like this scoop's all mine.' Miss Suit sniffs and stands up.

'Scoop?' My frown deepens and becomes a scowl as she replies.

'This will go viral in no time, you watch.'

Now I'm cross. I stand up and face her.

'Why would you want to invade someone's privacy just to humiliate them? I didn't think you worked for the gutter press. It's no one else's business what she does on holiday.'

Miss Suit backs away, looking startled at my strict telling off. She slinks off without another word.

'Pfft. I hate people like that with no morals, don't you?' I sit back down, possibly with smoke billowing from my ears. 'Should I tell security?'

Prince Charming raises his eyebrows a little and nods slowly. 'Don't worry, celebrities usually have their own security. She won't get near.'

'I hate unscrupulous journalists that are all about sensationalism and scandal. They give us all a bad name. Ugh. I hate that Mr Todgers called me a journalist in front of everyone at the meeting earlier. I couldn't think of anything worse.'

Prince Charming looks confused. 'You're not a journalist?'

'No! Well, yes, but... I'm nothing like her.'

He stares at me intently, his eyes narrowing as he studies my face. I sink down, realising I've been ranting. He stands up and bows his head towards me. 'Sorry, Miss Jackson, I'm afraid I have to go. I'm very sorry.'

Oh no, and now I've frightened him away. My head drops, but I raise my eyes and meet his. 'Cally.' I give a shy smile.

'Cally.' He smiles, and as he strolls away with his pile of books, he looks back at me and winks.

Winks! He just winked! At me! I stare after him, feeling... I don't even know... but he knows my name! And he smiled... with dimples! Shakira, Shakira! What a difference a day can make!

Butterflies

After lugging my body out of the shower, I sit on the fluffy stool at the ornate golden dressing table. I seem to be covered in stinging scratches and have a bruise on my leg. And I still feel shattered – having fun is hard work.

I don't let Lexi see me huffing at my reflections in the three mirrors – positive body image and all that being-a-good-parent stuff. I survey my face. When did I start looking so old? My youthful glow disappeared without me noticing. My eyes look a dull grey, and the size of these bags underneath would make Mary Poppins jealous. If only they were filled with money.

And all these lines – what was it Ben called them? *Laughter canals. Canals?* Maybe that's why I've been happy to disappear into an invisible middle-aged woman. Gone are the days of *if you've got it, flaunt it.* It's far easier to fade into the background than be visible and ignored.

Here, rubbing shoulders with the rich and beautiful, I'm starting to think that if I make an effort, maybe I could look a little more *beauty* and a bit less *beast*. I don't want people, especially a certain gorgeous prince, to see me as a frumpy old woman. I want to be a yummy mummy.

It was just a wink. An innocent, friendly wink. But at my age, I'll take what I can get. Why he was suddenly friendly, I have no idea, but it gave me a rush. Maybe it's Miss Suit he doesn't like. Ugh, I should win an award for my over-thinking skills. What is wrong with me? Why can't I shake this man out of my head? Actually, I think I know. Sadly, a wink is the most male attention I've received in far too long; I'm invisible as a woman to Ben. And it's fun! It's been so long since I've felt attracted to someone.

I don't want to imagine never experiencing romance ever again. Never going through those first few heady months of palpitations and desire and daydreaming. That's the best part of a relationship, the honeymoon period. Not twenty years later, still picking up their dirty laundry to put in the basket because they can't be bothered and without any thanks because all housework is done by some magical fairy that comes and tidies up after them. And then they forget your birthday because they've only been around for twenty previous birthdays, so how could they possibly be expected to remember?

I roughly towel dry my hair and study the range of complimentary bottles of health and beauty. I moisturise my neglected skin and slather my body in a whipped cream that smells good enough to eat. It leaves a light sheen that sparkles in the sunlight. I even apply some mascara and tinted lip balm, and finish with a spritz of a much-needed *wake up and smile* body perfume. Hopefully, I've upped my yummy-mummy quotient a fraction.

'Are you wearing make-up?' Lexi looks up from her book, astonished.

'A little bit.'

'What's the special occasion?'

'We're on holiday!' I almost convince myself. *Get a grip, Cally! I just need an interview so I can do the work I'm here to do.* 'Ready, Lex? Let's go.'

***

We queue outside the ballroom for this morning's first activity: a dance lesson to prepare for the ball at the end of the week.

The grand hall, adorned with sparkling chandeliers and gleaming hardwood floors, is full of male and female dancing staff ready to partner up with guests – all wearing black cropped tops and leggings.

When we get to the front of the queue, Lexi immediately disappears inside. I'm left in the doorway with Prince Charming, who welcomes everyone as they enter.

We stand face to face, and I can already feel the heat in my cheeks. He has a teasing quirk at the corner of his mouth, and I'm clearly imagining things, but it seems like his eyes slide up and down my body with a flirtatious look on his face. I can't cope with seeing Prince Charming's ripped biceps, abs, and, um, legs on display, and have to look away. Miss Suit is hovering in the corridor behind me, and I turn to her to break the tension. 'Are you coming to join us?'

'Some of us have work to do,' she snarls. 'We can't all play around being a hot mess.' She flicks her hair before flouncing off.

I throw my head back with a raucous laugh. 'She thinks I'm hot!'

'Well, you are hot, Cally,' Prince Charming says in his cool, matter-of-fact tone while flashing a mischievous smile at me.

I die.

The end.

He gives a light-hearted chuckle and steps aside for me to enter the ballroom. I float over to Lexi in a trance. That. Was. Sizzling.

Guests are split into pairs and small groups with a member of staff to instruct. Lexi and I are matched with a lovely, patient woman who I recognise as one of yesterday's fairies. Still dazed, I try to focus on my feet moving the right way at the right time – they make it look so easy on *Strictly*. Lexi picks it up immediately, whereas I keep crushing her little toes.

Then we have to learn about body posture, head and eye positions, and hand placement. Seriously? How do they expect me to concentrate on hands and heads and feets or whatever when Prince Charming just told me I'm hot?

Just as I'm nearly getting the hang of moving the correct foot, our small groups are disbanded and we have to shuffle along to find new partners. I daren't look to my left; I can already feel his presence and I'm already flustered. I don't need his muscles in my face to put me off these complicated dance steps. But of course, I want nothing other than his muscles in my face. Scrap the dancing. Oh Shakira, here goes...

I shift along and my gaze remains firmly at our feet, arms glued to my sides. He reaches for my left hand and places it on his bare shoulder. It is official; we have physical contact. I am actually touching his naked skin. He puts one hand on my back and lifts my chin with his finger. I don't know when I last took a breath.

'Cally,' he says softly. I finally look up through my lashes into his dark eyes. His large hand takes hold of mine, and with an electrifying glint in his eye, he stares at me for a long moment, making me want to whimper. Then, 'Head up, shoulders back,' he says in strict instructor mode. 'Hold your core muscles in tight.'

What core muscles? I don't think I have any.

'Now, back left, side, together. Right forward, side, together. And again...' Argh! We're moving!

My dance teacher is amazing. I'm looking into his eyes, following his instructions, and I start to get the hang of it. A huge grin spreads over my face, and I can't help bursting out, 'I'm waltzing! Woohooo!'

Prince Charming smiles down at me, and my shoulders relax now that I can do these few steps. And then something inside snaps or mends, I'm not sure which. My nerves dissipate, and I appreciate the fact I am dancing with *the Golden Adonis* and I'm going to relish every single minute.

I make no attempt to hide that I'm taking in the features of his gorgeous face – his all-consuming, half-moon eyes framed by strong brows, and his straight hairline and unfairly perfect skin, as though ageing has passed him by. Is it wrong to want to lick someone's cheekbones? And neck? I inhale every curve of the muscles on his chest and arms. My lips almost touch his skin, and it feels like the most incredible torture. My fingers mischievously squeeze his shoulder, and I suck in my cheeks trying to stop a cheeky grin. He playfully flexes his muscles in return, which makes me giggle.

'Apart from nearly drowning, did you enjoy the spa yesterday?' He curls his lips on one side, conjuring a bewitching dimple, but his playful teasing doesn't make me fluster this time.

'Yeah, I definitely saw something that took my fancy.' My sass is immediately replaced by a look of disbelief. I *did not* mean to say that out loud. Dammit!

He laughs, steps away, and claps his hands. He instructs us all to stand in a big circle, and Lexi comes running over to my side. It's time for Prince Charming to reward the guest who has made the most effort and progress during the lesson. Their prize is the last dance with the prince himself.

The music begins and Prince Charming spins in the middle of the circle, scanning the guests as he makes his decision. He stops when he is facing me. My heart leaps and my cheeks flush. He doesn't break eye contact as he slowly steps towards me. I'm surprisingly not nervous, more excited and chuffed to bits.

He's a step away and holds out his hand. As I raise my hand to take his, his arm jerks in a different direction. He gives me a wink and takes Lexi's hand, asking her for the pleasure of this last dance. His teasing makes me laugh, and it's wonderful to see how surprised and delighted Lexi is. She waltzes perfectly, beaming the whole time. When the music ends, Prince Charming bows and she curtsies to loud cheering and clapping from the group. My proud mummy heart swells.

'The final phase of your dance training is... to follow me...' Prince Charming says, leading us all out of the ballroom as if he's the Pied Piper. He leads us through a small woodland to a beautiful meadow that looks like a picture postcard, speckled with colours swaying in the gentle breeze.

The group gathers at the edge of the expanse of greenery. Prince Charming gives us further instructions: 'Now go, dance, play, have fun!'

Soft music plays through speakers hidden in the trees that are dotted around the field, and the group disperses, with each family finding their own space. Lexi and I look at each other, unsure how to dance to classical music. We look to the staff for inspiration.

The figures dressed in black stand out against the brilliant greens and yellows of the grass in the sunshine. They run and leap and tumble and cartwheel. Lexi can cartwheel, but I'm pretty sure I would snap if I tried.

'Look at them!' Lexi points to some figures in the distance performing gravity-defying flying, spinny, cartwheel-type moves. I recognise one of the figures immediately and watch Prince Charming kick his leg out in a circle as if his foot is painting a rainbow over his head.

'Wow!' That man's got some moves. He is F. I. T. with strength, suppleness, and stamina. I flap some cool air under my t-shirt; it's suddenly got rather hot.

Lexi and I hold hands and skip through the long grass. It's fun! I can't remember the last time I skipped, and I had forgotten how speedy it can be.

We pretend to be unicorns and gallop over to a tree, where we begin to let loose and shake out our limbs. We skip around the tree and then twirl into the wide space, frolicking without a care for others' opinions or expectations. Lexi does forward rolls and cartwheels. I twirl and sway, embracing the fun and exhilaration of feeling... free... for the first time in forever. My arms join in with dramatic flourishes and I become a child again, dancing like a butterfly.

We twirl with our arms out to the sides, giggling as we get dizzier and dizzier. I grab her hand, and with our heads still spinning, we tumble into a sea of tall daisies and buttercups. We land in a big hug and lie cuddling, giggling and catching our breath. Surrounded by flowers with the soft grass tickling our skin, we gaze up at the cloudless sky. It's a moment I will cherish forever.

***

When we return to the resort's centre, we find signposts directing us to a *Butterfly Garden Party*. We follow yet another new pathway through the trees and arrive at an archway of balloons and lanterns and sparkles. Lexi and I both gasp at the garden beyond. Hundreds of white butterflies flutter around beds of vibrant flowers, and bubbles float in the breeze. It's like all the resort's magic has been carefully curated into one perfect setting, and my chest feels ready to burst with happiness.

The catering ninjas have done an outstanding job of assembling magical butterfly-themed tables in the centre of the lawn. Floating above each chair are helium balloons filled with confetti, with butterfly wings hanging on the chair backs for us all to wear.

Lexi runs forward to select the wings she likes best and takes the seat. I put on my pink sparkly wings and sit down next to her. I love that all the fairy-tale characters join us for lunch and chat with the children. But why did she have to like the wings so close to where a quickly-changed-into-costume Prince Charming was sitting? Three seats along on the opposite side.

Laughter and conversation flow as we all make our lunch selections from the cheese boards spaced along the table. The cheeses and biscuits are cute butterfly shapes, and there are cookies baked with edible flowers on top that look too pretty to eat. Each place setting has a glass of homemade lemonade filled with a rainbow of fruits. The caterers are tremendously skilled in making fruits and vegetables look irresistible, even to my darling fussy pants. She hasn't mentioned fries even once since we've been here. So all I need to do back home is have an unlimited imagination and a few extra hours in the day. No problem.

I try to resist glancing over. I really do. But I'm intrigued that he has different food specially prepared. And my knowledge of Asian cuisine is shamefully lacking, so really I'm looking over for educational purposes.

He pops large slivers of meat into his mouth. The way he enjoys his food hypnotises me into watching his every mouthful. My inner wannabe vegan has disowned me, and I would be repulsed if it was Ben. But there's just something about his lips, the way he slurps those noodles, how he closes his eyes, savouring each bite… that distracts me from eating. My head leans to the side and I find myself stroking the silky table runner, watching him lick his lips, biting my lower lip in response. His eyes flick up, meeting my gaze, bursting my bubble of infatuation. I spin away and stare at my plate. *He caught me staring!* I scream in my head.

My chest is tight and I forget to breathe. Oh no, I hope Lexi hasn't noticed me drooling over a man who isn't her dad. I glance up to check on her, and my eyes accidentally slide towards him again. And he's looking at me. With an amused expression. With cheeks flaming, I shield my eyes with my hand and nibble at a cookie.

At the end of lunch, Lexi runs off to get an ice cream while we all leave the table and begin to gather for the next activity to start. She returns holding an ice cream cone. 'Mum, can you come with me?'

'Of course, where are we going?'

'To see Prince Charming.'

High-alert-heart-in-mouth mode instantly switches on. She grabs my hand and drags me towards the crowd, snaking a path through. 'There!' She lets go and rushes over, tapping him on the arm.

He turns around and smiles brightly at my little girl. I fake a calm smile and join her, breathing rapidly.

'This is for you.' She holds out the cone, vanilla ice cream dripping down the sides.

'Thank you very much!' he replies with a big smile.

'I wanted to thank you…' Awww, my heart swells, but…

'For being so nice and friendly… and for picking me to dance… and for making my mum smile a lot.'

And… there it is, that's what I was afraid of – her saying something innocently that totally embarrasses me. He smirks at me and I have to look away, my cheeks burning.

'You are welcome.' He drops to one knee to talk to Lexi at her height. 'Thank you for accepting my request to dance.' He leans closer and whispers, 'You are my favourite dance partner.' He puts his finger to his lips. 'Shhh.' He winks, and she beams brighter than ever.

'And I'm happy I make your mum smile.' He grins up at me, eyes twinkling.

My cheeks are on fire. Lexi looks at me curiously. 'Mum, why have you gone red?' There she goes again, and now my cheeks are incinerating, my whole body hot and tingling.

'Time to go!' I wipe the beads of sweat from my hairline while Prince Charming crinkles his nose and laughs. Why do these things always happen to me? I sigh and steer Lexi away. His eyes burn into my back as we join the gathering group of families. Without meaning to, I glance back over my shoulder. Our eyes lock just as his long tongue licks dripping ice cream from his hand. Is he teasing me? I think I may faint.

Find Strength in Solitude

Time to do some real work and start earning our free holiday. Nanny P accompanies Lexi to the afternoon kids' activity, and I find the garden cafe. Considering we've been here for three days, it's amazing that there are still new places to discover.

I take a seat in the beautiful garden patio cafe overlooking the pool – which looks so inviting in this heat. But today's hot-desk is perfect when I could be stuck in a stuffy office back home. Shaded from the midday sun by a wooden pagoda's canopy of leaves and curtain of pink wisteria strands – it's divine. I breathe in the lovely fresh air and give a nod of thanks to the gods of work environments.

I take out my notebook to jot down some questions ready for my imminent interview with Cinderella. I tap my pen repeatedly on the table. What do I ask my child-hood hero? It's strange to meet her now as an adult. As a kid, I identified with her suffering at home; I dreamed with her, shared her hopes for a happy ending. Do I even believe in happy endings anymore? Once upon a time, I thought I had found my *One True Love*, but that happy ending fizzled out long ago.

What do I need to know for my review? I shudder and throw down my pen, confiscating it from myself; Ben is so annoying when he taps his pen all the time. I'm usually more prepared than this – what have I been doing since we got here? I look around at the cafe's hanging lanterns and shabby-chic mis-matched furniture, getting inspiration to create an outdoor office in my garden. Then she arrives.

Cinderella's presence commands the cafe, not only because she's in full costume, but because she simply radiates magic. As she comes closer, I turn back into a little girl in complete awe. She is petite and stunningly beautiful. And she is wearing the blue dress I yearned for when I was young. The dress I pored over for so many hours as I read her story over and over and longed for my own fairy godmother to appear.

She greets all the guests in the cafe, exuding charm.

'Cally? How lovely to meet you.' She holds out her white-gloved hand. I stand to welcome her and shake her silky hand, so wonderstruck that it takes me too many seconds to reply.

'Cinderella, the pleasure is all mine.'

As she sits down, a waitress runs over to take our order.

'Two Americanos.' She orders *for* me and doesn't say please, but it's not every day you meet your idol for coffee. 'Please, call me Taylor.'

'So, Cin– Taylor, how does it feel to play the role of Cinderella?' I'm sitting forward, hanging on to her every word.

'It's a dream come true. And of course, the story of Cinderella teaches us to believe in ourselves and our dreams.' Her voice is sweet, and she has a warm, mild manner. I want to *be* her.

'Awww, that's lovely.' Our coffees are set on the table in front of us. I suppose I can try it black.

'And how is it working with the children?'

'I love children; they are all so sweet and adorable.' She sits demurely with her hands in her lap, a smile permanently on her lips. I take a sip of my coffee. Bitter and yuck, but I smile.

'What's your background? How did you find yourself here?' I ask with my pen poised.

'I'm from a small town in the middle of nowhere, but I've always loved performing. I'm like Cinderella in many ways: I'm very hard-working and determined.' She puts her hand to her chest and looks skywards. 'But I had a dream.' Her bright blue eyes twinkle. 'I'm full of hope and I always believed in myself. And…' She dips her head coyly, drawing me in. 'I'm kind-hearted and gentle, and I always see the best in people.' She looks up through fluttering eyelashes.

No, no, no. This doesn't feel right at all. I glance down for a split second to see my next question, but she is already saying, 'Thank you so much for coming to see me; it has been a joy talking to you. I must now rush back to my adoring guests.' Taylor stands and curtsies. My lips form the start of several different words, but I'm too taken aback to know what to say. She is already strutting off as I shift my chair backwards, and she's gone before I can stand. 'Thank you, bye,' I call out to the empty space where she stood. I slump in my seat, scratching my scalp, not quite sure what just happened.

What was that? Flummoxed, I sit there alone for a few minutes and then signal to the waitress that I would like some cream. It was like she had swallowed a *How to be Cinderella* textbook. I may as well have read her transcript myself. Everything she said sounded like a rehearsed spiel. The whole interview was an act, a sham, and a total waste of time.

The waitress brings a small jug of cream and some sugar to the table and takes Taylor's full cup that she didn't touch. I notice the waitress doesn't ask if the cup is finished with – like this wasn't the first time Taylor had done an interview in two seconds.

My disappointment feels as bitter as the taste of my coffee. I sulk back in my chair. I need a walk to clear my head.

Meh, she wasn't the real Cinderella.

***

I wander aimlessly, not ready for an earful of children, following a path around a high boxed hedge. I come to a gap where a huge, ornate, gold-rimmed frame stands, with simple lettering on a white background reading, *Find strength in solitude.* It strikes me as a bizarre message for a family resort, and it lingers in my mind as I explore what is on the other side of the tall hedges.

I've stumbled across a secret garden, a little piece of serenity in the middle of a loud, busy holiday resort. Following the stepping stones, I wind along the spiral path amongst tall ferns and trees like bushy palm trees. A wander through this peaceful oasis is just what I need – listening to the birdsong, musing, *Find strength in solitude.*

I don't get it. The last few years, I've been in solitude. Ben might have lived in the same house, but I've felt alone. And I certainly haven't felt strong. In fact, my marriage, that loneliness, has sucked all my strength away.

That thought triggers memories from a couple of years ago when I had daily thoughts of divorce. Long-forgotten memories that hit like a rush of dizzying blows. I become unsteady on my feet and sag down on a stone bench. I was struggling with going from being independent with a great job to being a stay-at-home mum with no personal income, wholly reliant on Ben. I remember how that lack of financial independence knocked my self-worth, and I lost myself. I was trapped. Ben kept having to work away from home, and at first, he would come home like a different person – so loving and attentive. But his efforts dwindled over time. Nowadays it's a relief when he works away, and he doesn't even bother to make up new excuses for working late. In fact, he pretty much ignores me. I shudder and need to keep moving.

As I walk, I recall telling myself it was better for Lexi that her parents stay together. I hug my arms around my body, reliving the fear that she may never forgive me if I ripped her family apart. So I never allowed my mind to bring up the D word again, even at the times when our home life was unbearable.

That was when my spirit broke. When I closed off my feelings and my heart turned to ice. My needs went painfully unmet, so I surrendered to the emotional deprivation. I was of no importance, and I became nothing. Felt nothing.

But maybe I'm not cold-hearted? What if I just feel cold towards Ben? I kick at the gravel, now feeling… angry? Resentful? Of course, I still did everything I could for Lexi, but I was a shell of the person I once was. I continue along the path, blinking back tears, realising I've been that shell ever since. I've been numb. Where did *I* go?

I walk into an area where bright sunshine spills through the shady leaves. It's like a light bulb beginning to brighten in my mind. Perhaps strength comes when solitude is your own choice. If I chose to be solitary, I might not feel powerless and vulnerable like I so often do being married.

I sit down on a sunny patch of grass and roll back my hunched shoulders. Being here, now, I sense my heart beginning to thaw. Letting myself go at the parade, dancing, twirling in the meadow with Lexi – these are glimpses of the old me peeking through. Maybe I needed a new view to see clearly, some space to notice how toxic my life has become, and to breathe fresh air to recognise I've been suffocating. I don't want to speak (or think) too soon, but maybe my spark is starting to light up again.

I watch some little fish swimming in their pond while my thoughts swim in my mind. I untie my ponytail and lift my face to the sun. Shaking my hair loose, my white – I mean, pale-gold – highlights shine in the sunlight. Then, leaning back, I spot something out of the corner of my eye... an old stone wishing well.

Strolling over, I pull a coin from my purse and toss it down the well. I know exactly what I want to wish for, although I can barely get myself to say the words out loud. Hell, I can barely allow myself to even think this way. I take a deep breath. 'I wish for love. I want to be in love and to feel loved and wanted.' I speak quickly, before I lose my nerve. 'I don't want to be irrelevant anymore.'

It feels good – almost a relief to release my wish into the well, and more wishes come bubbling to the surface.

'And I'd like to feel seen, and supported, to have someone to share the load with, someone who will take the lead sometimes and make decisions, someone I can rely on.'

I tap my finger on my lip and look up to see the birds flying free in the sky above me. 'Sorry, does that count as one wish?' I ask the inanimate well. I drop a couple more coins in the water, just in case. 'Oh, and some passion and excitement. That's not too much to ask, is it?' I shake out all the coins from my purse to be on the safe side.

Crunching from behind makes me spin around, heart racing. One of the yummy mummies from the spa clips past in her high heels, pushing her designer pram along the stony path.

'Treat yourself to a new wardrobe and bag yourself a sugar daddy, honey,' she chirps. I can't tell if she is imparting genuine advice or if she's mocking me.

'I'll think about it.' I chuckle back, dying inside, knowing I will be the topic of her friends' next gossiping session. Was I really saying my wishes out loud?

Once she is out of sight (and earshot), I brave the depths of my bag to search for one more coin. *I don't want to swap one old codger for another.* I must find another coin quickly so I can add to my list of requirements. An image of Mr Todgers as a sugar daddy pops into my mind. A cold shiver runs up my spine, and I empty the contents of my bag on the grass.

On my hands and knees, I sift through tissues, several of Lexi's hairbands, a sticky lollipop, a packet of crumbs that were biscuits in their previous life, pen lids. No coin. The closest I have is a button that my coat has lost hope of me ever sewing back on. I shove it all back in but, undefeated, rummage through the crumpled receipts in my purse (my highly efficient accounts filing system). I can't risk getting what I wish for if I haven't been specific. Eventually, I resort to dropping in a £10 note. I watch it flutter down into the water.

'Sorry, me again. Can I just add,' I whisper, 'young, gorgeous, funny, kind... and someone who wants to spend time with Lexi and is willing to act like a dad should.'

Now get me away from this thing before I bankrupt myself.

I feel lighter, happier, and accomplished, like I've just done something pretty courageous. I keep walking and have a new little spring in my step.

There are no flowers in this little part of the fairy-tale world, only greenery. It's like the garden is saying not to focus on external beauty, but to appreciate the beauty of the journey as you travel deeper into the centre. Or something like that.

Further along the little path, I notice that I'm humming. What is this tune? Something about how birds suddenly appear when you're near. Where on earth did this romantic part of me spring from? I blame Prince Charming. He is reigniting long-forgotten passions. I can sense parts of myself reawakening, parts that have been buried by motherhood and denied in marriage. I don't want to think *shrivelled up and full of cobwebs*, but the words pop into my mind.

I reach the centre of the garden – a small island. I hurry over the wooden bridge lying across a moat filled with koi carp, and amongst the leafy planting here on the central island, I spot flowers! Beautiful, deep-red blooms that I don't recognise but adore. It's like finding the inner beauty.

I follow the stepping stones around the trees into a circular area of grass with a stone bench in the middle. Simple, sunny, and sublime. This really is the perfect location for a little al fresco work time.

I perch on the bench, notepad on my knee and pen in hand. See, Mother, you said my part-time writing job was just a pretentious hobby that would never amount to anything, but I knew I could make it. Look at me now, here in paradise – I even look like a real writer! Where are those photographers when you need them?

Across the top of the page, I write:

Fairy-Tale Wonderland
A Review

Over the next few hours (an estimate that is probably nowhere near accurate, but certainly feels that way), I re-read the title several million times trying to decide how to begin the first sentence. Words fail me. After all that time, all I have managed to add is *First Draft* and *by Cally Jackson*. But before I admit defeat, I take a short stroll to refocus on my spectacular surroundings. I watch the fish, smell the flowers, and listen to the birds, soaking in their inspiration as well as a little sunshine.

It occurs to me that people must be inspired to write poetry at times like this – when they're so overwhelmed by the beauty of the moment, their feelings have to spill onto paper. While I have never experienced a moment like this before, nor written a poem since my school days, I feel inspired to capture the essence of simply being. Nothing but me and my pen, my revolutionary new thoughts, breathing in the calm of nature.

My fingers tingle, ready to create my masterpiece. I am channelling Mother Nature and allowing my feelings to simply flow...

> *I wish you were here,*
> *and not just in my mind.*
> *It's moments like this*
> *that I wish you were mine.*
>
> *You're all I that I dream of,*
> *you're all that I need.*
> *I picture your abs and,*
> *hot damn, think I've peed.*

'Mum!'

I jump clean out of my skin and spin around, shoving my scrawl into my bag.

'Lexi! And... Prince Charming?'

'I got a tummy ache and felt sick,' Lexi calls, clinging on to Prince Charming's neck as he piggybacks her towards me. I jump up to check on her. 'Are you all right?' There are no tears, no vomit stains. He lowers her to the ground, concern chiseling his godlike features, and she skips off to pick a flower.

'Lexi? Your tummy?'

'It feels better now,' she sings.

Prince Charming and I look at each other. 'I'm so sorry.' I shrug. 'I think she enjoys having your attention.'

'That's all right.' He stands with his hands behind his back and gives a sympathetic smile. 'Lots of children latch onto the characters here when a parent is absent.'

I dip my head and sigh. 'He's not exactly absent, just not around much, and even when he is home, he's emotionally distant.' I speak absent-mindedly, still attuned to my inner thoughts and feelings. It feels wrong to talk about Ben, and I find myself covering my wedding ring with my other hand. He's from the other side of the resort gates. The life I don't want to think about.

'Absent from your holiday here,' Prince Charming clarifies with a quiet inflection. 'I didn't mean to pry.'

'Ah. Yeah.' I grimace and flinch back to *this* present moment. Of course he wouldn't be referring to the state of our home life. Idiot. My eyes flick up to his. 'Sorry, you're too easy to talk to,' I mumble with a shy smile. But he doesn't seem uncomfortable. 'I bet all the guests must open up to you.'

He looks at me with kind eyes and a warm smile. 'I'm a good listener.'

'Shall we?' Ever the gentleman, Prince Charming places his hand about an inch away from my lower back as he shepherds me back out of the Secret Garden to join the children's activity.

'Sorry for interrupting your work.'

'Oh, that's no problem.' I fidget with my bag, immediately wanting to burn the poetry disasterpiece scrunched inside. 'How did you find me?'

'Lexi said you were at the cafe. I had a feeling you might come here.'

'I think it's my favourite part of the whole resort.'

'Mine too.'

Our eyes meet as we both smile and my insides flutter with affection. This is my favourite moment of our whole holiday.

'I didn't get my book.'

My silly moment of besotted bliss is interrupted by Lexi's sad little voice as she runs in between me and Prince Charming, taking hold of our hands.

'What book, my darling?'

'We were doing a treasure hunt and I found the key in the suit of armour and we found a tower and the key opened the door! And inside there was a library and a secret hiding place and the book with the bow was the treasure. And I gave it to Nanny P to look after, but then I felt sick and I didn't get it back.' She exaggerates a frown.

'I will take you to get the book. Do you want another piggyback?' Prince Charming squats down for Lexi to climb on.

'That's very kind of you, thank you.' Oh my goodness, he's delicious – I mean, considerate.

'My dad never gives me piggybacks. Thank you, Prince Charming.'

It breaks my heart to hear my little girl say such things. Before Lexi jumps on Prince Charming's back, he turns to her and takes hold of her hand.

'Let me tell you a secret about dads.'

Lexi looks up to him with wide eyes, listening closely. As am I.

'Sometimes they get so busy that they don't get time to play. Isn't that sad?'

She raises her eyebrows and nods.

'But I promise your dad loves you more than anything, even if sometimes he forgets to show you.' His face is sincere, and he speaks his wisdom with such authority that Lexi accepts his truth with a satisfied smile.

'Now, in my duty as prince, it's piggyback time.' He presents his back, and she jumps on, her face bright and giggling as she throws her arms around his shoulders. He turns to me and winks. 'We have to give the lady what her heart desires.'

I don't even know if there was any hidden message aimed at me, but my legs turn to jelly and I want to do one of Lexi's theatrical fall-on-bed swoons.

***

Lexi and I finish our room-service dinner – giggling throughout, copying the shocked look on the waiter's face when he flamboyantly lifted the silver-domed cloches to reveal two plates of sausage, fries, and ketchup. She sits on her bed cuddling Princess Bear and the book.

'What's up, Lex? You look like you want to say something.'

'It's just that... because Nanny P helped me with the treasure hunt today and she helped me find the book...' She pulls her knees up to her chest, scrunching up her toes. 'Would you mind if Nanny P reads my story and puts me to bed tonight?'

'No, of course not.' I smile and sit down next to her to give her a cuddle. 'I'll phone reception and make the arrangements.'

'Are you sure you don't mind?'

'It's fine, my darling, but thank you for asking.'

Nanny P is quick to arrive and sits with Lexi to play games. Do these phenomenal staff members ever get any time off? I feel a bit guilty jumping in the shower, getting ready to go out and have time off myself. But I have a night off! I'm not sure if the butterflies in my stomach are excitement or nerves.

'All OK over there?' Nanny P notices me hovering in my dressing gown, staring at the wardrobe where the staff have hospitably hung my clothes.

'It's been so long since I've had a night out, I don't know what I should wear.'

'No rock-chick princesses!' Lexi yells as she joins me to help decide. 'Wear something pretty and sparkly.'

'You can't go wrong with a little black dress,' Nanny P suggests with a smile.

'Hmm, I don't think I own a dress. I'll just go with jeans and a nice top.' I dig out my only posh top – nothing fancy, but a bit smarter than a t-shirt.

Nanny P's face brightens, her enthusiasm shining through as she cheers me on. 'That will look lovely with some heels.'

'Oh, I only have sandals.'

'Lovely!' Nanny P is always so polite.

I take the outfit into the bathroom to change. I don't own any *going out* clothes; there's no need when I never go out. I look in the mirror and sigh. Oh well, this will have to do. The excited butterflies fly away.

Lexi's waiting outside the bathroom door, jumping up and down when I open it.

'I can do your make-up, Mum.'

'No thanks, Lex. I don't want to make a fuss.' I stroke her hair. Her little moments of kindness make me feel like Ben and I aren't totally screwing her up.

'What about this lip gloss that was in my gift basket?' She pulls it from her pocket.

I remember I'm supposed to be making an effort not to look like a frump. 'Go on then.' I give my hair a quick blast with the hairdryer and leave it down – my equivalent of making an effort with styling – and stick a bit of pink gloss on my lips. Lexi sprays me with perfume, covering us both in a bergamot haze. I give Lexi a kiss goodnight, and I'm ready to go out.

'Have a nice time, Mum.'

'Have fun! Stay out as long as you like,' calls Nanny P.

'Thank you, see you later. Be good, Lex, and don't stay up too late.'

***

I wander around the village square. I'm *out out*, young and wild and free. But not so young and not quite sure what to do with my freedom. The lights of the resort are striking against the night sky. I walk over to the tree of memories, is it? Dreams? Wishes? Whatever, it's beautifully lit and I sit on one of the benches beneath, watching the world go by.

The evening's family entertainment is over and children are being tucked up in bed, so it's mostly couples and a few families with older children wandering past. The atmosphere is cosy and intimate, apart from the just-married couple who were on the bus here. They're wearing matching Mr and Mrs t-shirts and having a hushed argument outside the bar. I know I thought their smiles wouldn't last, but I didn't think they'd only last a couple of days.

Street performers are dotted around the village this evening, entertaining guests with music and comedy. From my vantage point, I can see a trio of clowns doing a crazy balancing act and a gold-painted man seemingly hovering in mid-air.

The longer I sit by myself when everyone around looks happy, the more I feel a teeny-weeny bit miffed that Lexi wanted someone else to be with her for bedtime. I'm starting to think a night off alone isn't really much fun. I consider having a drink in the lounge bar, but I don't feel comfortable drinking on my own and I'm not in a chatty enough mood to meet couples. I could go for a stroll around the resort, but it's been a busy day and going for a walk without a dog seems like a waste of energy. I usually work once Lexi's asleep, or watch other people enjoying their fun and fulfilling lives on TV.

I miss my Barney dog, even with his dog breath and room-clearing farts. At least he keeps me company. What do I do if I'm not doing mum things? Who on earth am I when I'm just me? My party balloon just deflated.

I wander to the private courtyard – the only area I've found to smoke, hidden away from the rest of the resort – through the door of do-you-like-cheese shame, and down the path to the seating area of chocolate-smudge shame. I stop dead when I turn the corner, and shrink back to the shadowy path. Prince Charming and Cinderella are sitting at the table. Drinking. Laughing. Crinkly-eyed, dimply-smile laughing.

I pause in the shadows. I don't want to interrupt. They're colleagues, so it makes sense they socialise together after work. Even if he is sitting on top of the table right in front of her, instead of on a seat. With several shirt buttons undone, looking relaxed and happy and having fun. So why does my chest hurt? And why do I feel physically sick? How can I possibly be feeling jealous? He's not mine. Ah. I realise my mistake at the wishing well. I didn't wish for someone who's available.

I creep back up the path and quietly exit with a deep sense of unease. I miss the familiar comfort of reading bedtime stories with Lexi, snuggling her up in bed and kissing her good night before wrapping myself in a duvet and hiding from the world.

I go up to our room and let Nanny P go early. Lexi's already fast asleep. I kiss her forehead gently so as not to wake her. She looks adorable all snuggled up with

Princess Bear under her arm. I remove the book from her hand and release a silent sigh.

I climb into bed, but don't feel sleepy. Lying in the dark, my mind is all over the place. I don't even *do* feelings. How dare someone come along and not only turn me into a mushy mess of soppy romantic feelings, but also make me feel envious of a sweet, naïve young girl? A beautiful young woman with no laughter canals, a perfect figure, and who wears dresses with high heels. And it hurts, which is completely absurd. What next? I give her a poisoned apple? I amuse myself, even if I do get my fairy tales muddled, but the sharp sting of jealousy keeps a smile from my lips.

And oh, what a joy to discover that after all these years, I am still the same stupid, lovesick, heartbroken teenager, but now with the face of a mature woman. Who knew?

But I'm fine. Everything is going to be fine. Lexi is all I need. I'll keep telling myself that.

Topsy-Turvy

Lexi and I lounge by the pool drinking mocktails garnished with exotic fruit wedges and shiny, fringed umbrellas. Today is the day I'm actually going to start on my work.

'Why have I got to write a review anyway?' Lexi slams down her pen.

'I already explained, Lex. I think it would add a unique spin. The brochure doesn't mention what kids think of staying at the resort; it's important for kids to have their say too, don't you think?'

'Yeah, but it's so hard.' She huffs. 'And I want to play in the pool with my new friends.'

'I know. You can play once you've finished. You only need to write a few lines of what you think about your holiday.'

'Yeah, but like, what?' Lexi replies in an irritating nasally whine.

'Just imagine what you'll say to your friends when you're back at school.'

'Fine.' Hmm... her lips curl into a mischievous grin, but at least she's picked up her pen and started writing.

Lexi's right, though. With its lazy river and poolside trampolines for jumping into the water, this place looks awesome. Maybe I am mean – this isn't really the fun, relaxing mummy-and-daughter morning I would like. I understand her struggles and huffing for the past hour. I can't think how to put this amazing fantasy world into words. So far this morning, all I have come up with is one word: spectacular. The hotel? Spectacular. The entertainment? Spectacular. The whole fairy-tale experience? Spectacular. If I'm going to get this review finished, I really need to think of some other words to use.

Miss Suit was going into the resort owner's office when we passed this morning. She's obviously getting on with her interviews, whereas I only have Cinderella's useless spiel so far. But I'm pleased with my new idea for a different kind of review: capturing a guest's perspective, rather than all the other reviews that just detail a resort's features and services. That type can seem a bit robotic and serious, which doesn't suit this place at all. Judging by Miss Suit's wicked witch expression earlier, and her wanting to out the famous woman at the beginning of the week, I wonder if her review will be as poisonous as she comes across as.

I have scheduled my meeting with Mr Todgers, but I'm not sure I'll get to meet with Prince Charming. I just want my review to be the best I can make it; I don't want to let anyone down. But there's so much riding on this assignment that I'm scared to start. It's not even that I'm particularly ambitious, it's just that I've sacrificed so much, for so long, taking care of my family; now I have a chance to prove myself as a person and show I have some value. And that promotion and pay rise would give me options I haven't been able to consider before.

So. Much. Pressure.

It doesn't help that everywhere I look there's an exciting way to procrastinate. And even then, my annoying mind constantly slides back to *him*. My brain does not approve of the distraction when it's already Thursday and I've only written one word. Maybe it's for the best that I'm too scared to ask him for an interview anyway, especially after the way he shut down Miss Suit's request.

'Mum, how would you describe our fairy day?'

Lexi's voice makes me jump, and I focus back on my little girl lying on her front, kicking her feet in the air. 'Hmm, enchanting?'

'And what about the magical banquet?'

'Spectacular?' I kick myself. I wish I could focus.

Phone! Oh my goodness! I can't believe I didn't think of it before. Have I really broken my addiction in just a few short days? I've loved not having notifications pinging every two seconds. I pull up my knees to sneak it out of my bag and check the thesaurus. It's not even switched on. *Ting ding a ding a ding!* it screams at top volume. So much for my covert mission.

'Mum!' Yes, yes, Lexi. I'm well aware.

'I better go somewhere less crowded. I'll be back in a minute with more words.'

'OK, but I've finished anyway, so I'm going to join the kids' club in the pool.' With a burst of energy, Lexi runs off to finally do fun things.

I tie a floaty sarong around my waist and walk around to the other side of the pool, to what appears to be a massive greenhouse. Pushing open the door, I enter a new world – a fantastic, topsy-turvy world. I step inside onto a bouncy, sky-painted floor, awed by the plants and flowers growing down from the glowing green ceiling. It's like entering an upside-down, bright, floral cave – with a waterfall where the water appears to magically flow upwards. It makes my brain spin. The trailing and climbing foliage creates the impression they're growing from the ground above and vibrant pink and purple flower stems hang low as though they are growing upwards. I can't tell what's real and what's not, and I have to say, it's spectacular.

I perch on a low wall behind a clump of fluffy, yellow, alien-looking flowers that give off whiffs of... ice cream? Sitting with my back to the walkway, I take out my phone. This time, I remember to put it on silent. I swipe away the hundreds of messages and email notifications – real life can stay on hold until I get home. No messages from Ben, I see. He obviously misses me as much as I miss him.

I begin to type *synonyms* into Google, but I am distracted by the camera in my hand. The temptation to take a quick photo of the amazing interior is too strong. I flip the camera view and recoil at my hideous thirty-two double chins showing on the low-angle screen, and quickly raise the phone to find a view of the magical upside-down waterfall.

There's a familiar navy blazer in the corner of the screen, and I zoom in to see Miss Suit. There's something shifty about her squinting eyes and the way she's talking into her phone behind her hand. I can hear her ominous cackling all the way from here. She looks like she's up to no good again, and I just don't like it. If I could dive into these bushes without all the other guests seeing me, and then crawl through those alien plants, I reckon I could find out what she's up to without her noticing...

Bikini and sarong aren't the best way to dress for such manoeuvres. As I start crawling through the alien bush, with yellow fluff sticking to my skin like camouflage, I wonder how my life has come to this. My palms are sweating and acting like a magnet for all kinds of petals and pollen. At least it smells nice. Stones are digging into my knees, and I'm desperately trying not to sneeze. I'm close enough to hear the malice in her tone, but not quite make out her words; I just need to commando crawl a little bit further.

'So that's what I'm focusing on now. This Prince Charming guy was massive all over South Asia. Why the hell would anyone go off grid to come here? He's got to be a much bigger scoop than this awful place.'

...

'You have no idea what it's like – kids everywhere, with their icky little fingers and the noise! It's horrendous.'

...

'Yeah, he won't interview, but I'll get him. I'll make one of them spill, don't you worry.'

Miss Suit finishes her call. I lay flat and try to meld into the rocks, closing my eyes tight. My blood is boiling. How dare she be planning something awful for Prince Charming? What did she mean, *go off grid* and *make them spill*? Who? Spill what? I wait for her to leave, not daring to take a breath.

'*Achoo!*'

Shit! I squash my face down further into the orange moss. Please, alien flower gods, don't let her catch me. I can't explain my way out of this one. Why couldn't my stupid nose hold that in for just another few moments? Oh god, this cunning plan could totally backfire. I could end up the one in serious trouble.

I count to twenty and bravely peer up. She's gone. I collapse back to the ground with a huge surge of relief and refill my lungs with lovely sweet oxygen. That was too close. Now I need to act quickly, before evil Miss Suit makes her gossiping *go viral*.

I can't face caterpillar crawling backwards, so I'll have to ride this one out. I stand up, snort moss out of my nose, rub the stones from my knees, and casually walk out of the flower bed as if all is normal. A nearby kid points me out to his parents. They stare but are either too surprised or polite to say anything. I brush off as much fluff as I can and walk back around to my little wall to sit down. There, all perfectly normal. Nothing to see here.

First things first – Google. I need to know what that dreadful woman was talking about. It's only now that I realise I only know him as Prince Charming, not his real name. No problem. The Internet is scarily intrusive, and within a minute I find his full career history, family background, and home address in Korea.

Han Jisung – Actor, Model, Cultural
Icon, South Korea

What? OMG! That is a vast back catalogue of K-dramas and movies. My phone can't translate the words quick enough. What the actual f…?

He's actual Asian A-list! Like, proper superstar!

There are a million and one photos of him looking gorgeous. Gosh, he's topless in this one, showing off his incredible physique and smouldering eyes, tongue at the side of his open mouth. I save the image to a private folder. For, ahem, research purposes.

It doesn't feel good spying on my life-saving-hero-slash-almost-friend-slash-acquaintance. I feel like a stalker, or worse still, a journalist like Miss Suit. Although, there is one good thing. Despite his youthful skin and no wrinkles whatsoever, he's older than he looks. And I'm extremely pleased to read that I'm nowhere near old enough to be his mother. In fact, he's only a few years younger than me. Maybe I should ask him for some skincare tips.

I obsessively scan through all the women he's pictured with – all stunning, perfectly groomed, short, petite, and oh so cute. All the complete opposite of me. My self-esteem drains away with each photo.

I scroll down pages and pages of articles, fan pages, videos, memes, and photos of him with different actresses and models. I can't see anything about why he would quit an impressive, award-winning career. But from the headlines, it seems he has dated every beautiful woman in Korea. There's not so much written about his acting; the majority seems to be commenting on his relationships and complaining he has closed his social media accounts.

What on earth happened? Now *I* am intrigued by what brought him here. But I'm sure he doesn't want his secrets splashed all over the media by Miss Suit.

I switch off my phone. I've seen enough. Miss Suit said she was going to focus her article on Prince Charming and not the resort – but I'm pretty sure she hasn't been invited here to take the place down. And the glee in her voice when she spoke about wanting to publish someone's secrets makes my skin crawl, however interesting and gossipy the scoop may be. Especially when they're Prince Charming's secrets. Well, not on my watch. I need to nip this in the bud, right now.

Leaving this topsy-turvy place, I catch a glimpse of myself that makes me stop to take a closer look. I peer in the mirror straight on, and my reflection is upside down, because of course. I tilt my head to read the upside-down words around its edge:

Mirror Mirror on the tree,

I'm much more than you can see.

'Exactly!' I burst out loud and quickly exit without checking if anyone noticed I'm talking to myself. Again.

There are no filters or fakery with me; what you see is what you get. No nasty surprises when I wipe off my make-up. Hmm, maybe a few when I take off my shapewear.

I make a speedy march inside to reception, where a stylish, mature woman with a silver-haired bob and piercing blue eyes stands behind the desk.

'Cally Jackson, isn't it?' She holds out her hand with a bright smile. 'We haven't had a chance to meet yet. I'm Diane, Diane Todgers. I think you've met my husband?'

'Pleased to meet you.' I shake her hand. 'I wonder if we could have a quick chat?'

'Yes, of course, my dear.' Diane ushers me into her chic minimalist office. Being a snitch is quite nerve-wracking, but there's no point in me writing a great review of the resort if Miss Suit, with her larger readership, is going to trash the place or its staff.

We sit on the modern white couch, and I fill her in on what I heard Miss Suit say, leaving out the crawling-through-plants part. For good measure, I throw in details of the celebrity guest conversation from our first night here. Diane's friendly face pales, and her warm smile fades.

'Thank you for telling me this, Cally. I shouldn't say, but my husband had to give her a warning this morning about sneaking around the hotel trying to invade people's privacy.'

'That's awful.' I knew that sly fox couldn't be trusted.

With my good deed done for the day, and lots of work still to do, I keep the pleasantries short. As we both stand to leave the office, my eyes and mouth fly open and my cheeks burn when I notice the couch. Where I was sitting, the once-white couch is now bright yellow. I frantically rub off the fluff, but the yellow flower stains remain.

'I am so, so sorry.'

Diane waves off my mortification over the bright stain with a laugh. 'Don't worry at all, dear. We're not precious here – it's just a couch.' She pats my back and I find myself pulling her into a hug as I apologise again. I don't know where that came from. How unprofessional. I think it might have been me who needed a hug, with my mind so jumbled.

I leave Diane's office and pass Mr Todgers in the lobby. I become very aware that I am barely clothed when he watches me go around the reception desk, and feel quite uncomfortable under his gaze. I cross my arms over my bikini top and hurry back out to the pool.

With Lexi gone, mummy-and-daughter time lounging in the sun is sadly over. On her sun lounger is a page of writing with a big *THE END* forcefully underlined at the bottom. I slap my palm on my forehead. I forgot to check the thesaurus – the whole reason for my phone escapade. I'm useless.

I grab Lexi's paper and rest back on the lounger, curious to see what prompted my darling daughter's giggles as she was writing.

Review by Lexi age 9

Yo! Fairy Tail Wonderland holiday ressort is SICK bro. you feel like a princess IRL and get to dress up and dance and sing with all the squad of caracters and make BFFs. and dont even get me started on the ball - - - its gonna be LIT!!!!!!!!!

There is a fairy day when you play games with actual fairys. It is legit enchanting we had a magic bankquet. It was spectaculer

the food was cray and we did a dope treasure hunt and the swimmin pool is sweeeet!

Vibin here is Gucci and coming back is goals. but B.E.W.A.R.E. Parents play with you and when boomers join in OMG it is CRINGE but TBH it is nice to play with your fam and they smile a lot and are happy.

This holiday is GOAT!!!!!!!

Fairy Tale Wonderland is FIRE no cap

THE END

***

I give up on reviews for now. If my hair isn't pure white by the end of this week, it will be a miracle.

I drop my sarong to the ground and make my way down the sloping poolside to cool off.

I ignore the fluff and bits of plants floating from my body. I don't even care that people may misconstrue the yellowing water surrounding me. There is a lot to process.

So Prince Charming is a player – definitely not searching for his one true love. I'm certainly not interested in being yet another notch on his bedpost, if I got the chance, before being cast aside for his next conquest. Is

Cinderella one of those notches? Is that why they were drinking together last night?

I float on my back in the refreshing water and stare up at the perfect clear-blue summer sky. I'm glad I discovered what he's really like before I made a proper fool of myself. I should have known better.

The problem is my mind can use any topsy-turvy tactics to try to make me feel better about myself, but my heart knows the truth. It is easier to think badly of him rather than acknowledge my inadequacies in comparison to the women in his past. I could never compete. And he is so ridiculously far out of my league, I would never be good enough. I am never enough.

I swim a few strokes and stand under the waterfall springing from the rocks at the pool's edge. The cascading water hides the insecurities that escape from my eyes and trickle down my cheeks. I attempt to pack up these feelings and shove them back deep inside. As Lexi said, I've been married forever. I remember at first when I felt lucky that Ben deemed me good enough. When I accepted that ring, I never expected to face this pain and ugliness again.

***

Sunglasses on – more to dim the glare of my white legs than the scorching sun – I lie back on the sun lounger. Mrs Life-and-Soul joins her husband at a table across the pool – the first time I've seen her since Jacuzzi Bubble-Gate. It's cute how they look at each other with love; there is clearly a comfortable silence between them. He listens intently when she becomes animated and babbles something, replies a few words while looking at her adoringly, and holds her hand across the table.

The silence is icy between me and Ben. If I speak, he doesn't look up from his phone, and always denies knowing anything of our 'conversations'. I can't remember the last time we sat opposite each other, just the two of us, and I don't think Lexi has ever seen us hold hands.

Little Miss Life-and-Soul runs over to her parents. Her dad lifts her onto his knee, gives her a big hug, and feeds her a forkful of his cake. She smiles and chats away happily while my heart lurches painfully in my chest. My poor baby girl never gets Ben's undivided attention, no daddy-daughter days. She is missing out, the same way I did as a child, and she deserves better. Maybe I do too.

Mrs Life-and-Soul gets up and leaves her little family unit and walks around the pool. Towards me. Uh oh.

'Did you hear what happened? With that other reporter woman?' She speaks so fast it takes a moment to decipher her words.

'No?'

'Carted off by security! I just saw it happen in the lobby. Kicking and screaming, she was. All very unladylike.'

With a sharp intake of breath, I sit bolt upright. I don't know what to say.

'Hope *you* haven't been doing anything naughty!' She laughs, her hair bobbing up and down as if it were a separate entity.

I shake my head, feeling shocked, guilty, pleased, relieved, jumbled.

'You look sad, my love. Everything OK?' Mrs Life-and-Soul asks quietly, sitting on the side of Lexi's lounger.

'Yes... yes, thank you.' I shake away my thoughts. 'I'm fine, just thinking about what to write in my resort review,' I lie with a smile.

'I'm sure you'll have plenty of lovely things to say about the ball on Saturday. We chose our costumes this morning, got the old *beast* ready.' She nods back to Mr Life-and-Soul, laughing playfully. 'Have you chosen your outfit?'

'Not yet, but I've always dreamed of wearing a Cinderella dress.'

'How fun! Especially with a dishy prince on your arm.' She winks. 'It's fun to get lost in the fantasies here, isn't it?' She doesn't pause for breath, let alone wait for an answer.

'That Prince Charming is a hottie, isn't he? He and Cinderella look fabulous together.' She leans in closer and whispers loudly behind her hand, 'I hear they're doing it, you know, behind the scenes.' She laughs merrily, oblivious to the bombshell she's just dropped.

'Well, I'll leave you to it.' The bubbly woman whirls away as quickly as she arrived.

My mind is buzzing with all of today's new information. So they really are 'doing it'; Prince Charming really is a playboy. I should have guessed; after all, she is the fairest in all the land, or whatever. And Miss Suit's been kicked out. I want to hide in a tower for a hundred years and wait for this whole palaver to blow over. How come

I'm in a magical fairy-tale paradise feeling thoroughly disenchanted?

THURSDAY

Labyrinth of the Soul

Work is the last thing I feel like doing. I wander through the gardens for some *me time* instead, something I rarely have in real life. Lexi is enjoying playing with the other girls, acting out scenes from their favourite stories, and I trust Nanny P to supervise. The entertainment cast is putting on a show for the children later. Lexi will be happily entertained and Prince Not-So-Charming-After-All will be on stage, so there is no risk of bumping into him and feeling accidentally giddy. A slight wave of relief washes over me. I need a break from my muddled emotions.

No wonder you hear of people afflicted by a mid-life crisis buying a motorbike and riding off into the sunset, leaving all their problems behind. Or trading their partner for a younger model and starting afresh. Now I understand.

Or perhaps I'm looking at this all wrong. Maybe mid-life isn't a crisis, but more like an end of probation review, a 1:1 with the universe. *You've been here for forty years now. How are things going? Anything you'd still like to achieve or need to change?* There! Not scary at all. Just a little chat with the gods of being happy. I deserve to be a little bit happy, don't I?

According to social media, at my age, I'm supposed to be settled with a great career, wearing a twin set and pearls, and starting my menopause at any second. But, *plot twist!* Here I am, unhappily married and lusting after a holiday romance with a gorgeous Asian A-list superstar playing Prince Charming in a fairy-tale utopia.

Having a mid-life crisis is exhausting.

I just wish I knew what to do for the best for me and Lexi. Everything feels up in the air with no easy solutions in sight, no happy ending all wrapped up with a bow. For now, I'll have to leave it up to the help-me-sort-my-shit-out gods. Come on, universe, give me a sign!

This alone-time walk should feel like a treat, but I'm not very good company. I shake my head to come back to the present. I have been walking on autopilot and now have no idea where I am physically either. My sense of direction has never been a strong point. I am surrounded by tall trees blocking all views of recognisable points. It's beautiful to look at, but I would prefer not to be lost.

I continue further, hoping the view will clear and I can see where to go. The path narrows and the bushes on either side become long, immaculately trimmed cuboids. Straight ahead seems to be a hedge T-junction, and there's a large book on a stand decorated with trailing purple flower vines. Maybe it is a resort map? As I get closer, I see the book has only four words. This does not bode well.

The book displays arrows pointing left and right, with the words:

One Way Or Another

'That is not helpful,' I tell the book, propping my hands on my hips. The path in both directions looks exactly the same. Am I in a maze? I did not sign up for this.

Here goes nothing. I take lefts after rights after lefts until the path widens. Phew! I may have panicked too soon. There's a big stone fountain – I must be in the centre. I relax a little and enjoy the view of beautiful flower beds around the fountain bathed in the afternoon sun.

The base of the fountain is engraved with lettering. I circle around, reading:

Labyrinth of the soul –

Getting lost along the way

Is part of finding your own path

'Oh, give me a break.' Enough with the hippy-trippy nonsense. I don't want to be in a labyrinth; I just want to know the way out so I can get back to Lexi. I'm *delighted* to see, what, eight paths leading out from the fountain? The hedges are now all different heights. Is that supposed to be a clue?

Fine. I'll take the path with the lowest hedge. Within seconds, I completely lose track of directions and which paths I've already been down. I'm sure I'm going round in circles; I wish I had some breadcrumbs to leave myself a trail.

This. Is. Not. Fun.

I take another right. And... I'm back at the same fountain. I kick out at a flower bed. 'For fu– I am getting very irritated.'

I whisper an apology to the flowers and try to straighten a broken stem. OK, try again. I drag my feet through the gravel towards the tallest hedge path. Left, right, left. Aha! The hedges here are short and curved, with lovely planting in all shades of green. If I wasn't stuck, I might appreciate it. The correct path is still no clearer. I'm sure there must be a system for working out these things. Which is great if you know what the system is. Whoever designed this maze needs a good kick with a glass slipper.

More lefts, more rights, more paths, more flowers. This stupid maze is just like my muddled thoughts, twisting me this way and that. Then I come across a statue of a woman, almost hidden behind one of the hedges. She holds a scroll, which reads:

Sometimes the right path

is not the easiest

'What does that mean?' I yell at her. Of course, she doesn't reply. Why can't she be some kind of magical talking statue and help me out here? 'What do you want from me? A secret code? How do I know which path is right?' I slump to the rocky ground and remove a stone from my shoe.

I can't just give up or I'll be stuck here forever. No one knows I'm here. I don't even know where *here* is, or how long I've been here. My phone is back at the hotel, so I can't even call for a rescue helicopter or flying carpet – I'm not fussy.

I take a deep breath. Defeat is not an option. 'Come on, Cally, you can do it.' I get back up to my aching feet and carry on going – none the wiser, just taking one step at a time. One way or another, I have to find the exit. I turn the corner, and there in front of me... the damn central fountain.

I'm tired. And lost. And exasperated. And in a very bad mood. Note to self: next time, remember to pack survival snacks. I throw my arms up to the universe.

'Please, god of mazes, don't let me die here... or need to pee.'

As I balance on the edge of the fountain to rest my feet, the maze lights up in preparation for the sun setting. How long have I been stuck here? I must keep going before I have to make myself a bed out of leaves. Maybe there was a hidden emergency-send-a-search-party button on that statue? I retrace my steps, the paths now lit with little white lights along the ground.

I make a desperate search attempt all around the statue, press her nose, pull her finger, poke her in the eye. But there's nothing. I stand back, scowling at her stupid smiling face. *Sometimes the right path is not the easiest.* Well... if the right path isn't easiest, does that mean the left path *is* the easiest? So if I take all left turns...

***

Stepping back inside the Palace Hotel is like easing into a big, warm, welcoming hug, and I am comforted by the sight of the ladies' bathroom and the freshly baked cookies.

I emerge from the bathroom refreshed and smelling amazing thanks to the incredible array of lotions, potions, and spritzers offered in the bathroom's fancy free display. I could get used to this luxurious lifestyle where all my needs are preempted.

I pick a chocolate chip cookie, and as I'm wondering where I'll find Lexi, a pastel-pink blur zooms towards me. A flushed and flustered Thalia comes to a sudden halt beside me with Diane running closely behind her.

'Cally!' she splutters. 'Thank goodness you're back.'

Diane grabs my hand, trying to catch her breath to speak. I freeze.

'Lexi!' I yell. 'What's happened? Is she all right? Where is she?'

'She's fine, she's fine.' Diane pats my shoulder.

I exhale a huge, pent-up breath, dropping my shoulders as I try to get the panic to subside.

'It's your husband.'

'Ben?' Now the alarm bells ringing in my head are deafening. What's happened? Is my precious Barney dog OK? The house? Both women speak at once, but I manage to glean that Ben has been phoning constantly for hours trying to reach me.

Diane leads me quickly by the hand to a nearby inlet just off the corridor, sitting me down at the desk with an anxious pat. 'I'll get him on the line, dear.' Her heels click away down the hall, and in the distance I catch her hushed whisper, 'The poor thing, she looks ready to faint!' Her concern wraps around me like a blanket.

Seconds later, Thalia appears with a large tumbler of brown liquor and puts it in my hand. She pushes the old-fashioned telephone towards me.

'We are here for you,' she says before leaving me in privacy.

My heart is racing; I'm a nervous wreck. Memories of the last emergency call flood my mind. My colleague's hand clutching mine as I heard the news my dad had died. All the shock, confusion, and loneliness I felt then threatens to choke me now.

I down the unknown liquor while I wait for the phone to ring. It burns my throat and makes me cough, leaving my mouth ready to breathe fire. Why was I stuck in that stupid maze for so long? If I wasn't such an idiot, I would have been here, where I was needed.

I was packing to come here when I last spoke to Ben. I made a simple request for him to pick up his wet towel. He made out I was being unreasonable, and it turned into a huge row. I jump at the loud ring, my nerves frayed. I pick up the receiver with a trembling hand.

'Ben?' I can hear the quiver in my voice. 'What's happened?'

'About time! I've been trying to get hold of you all day. Where's my black shirt?'

'What? Why? What's happened?' The knot in my stomach twists as I wait for his reply.

'Why didn't you answer my calls?' He sounds more angry than anxious. I feel myself retreating even though

I haven't purposely done anything wrong, and my voice shrinks. 'I didn't have my phone on me.'

'Where's my black shirt? It's gone.'

A small, gaudy mirror between some silver candlesticks on the desk reflects my pale face, which is etched with a firm frown. 'Probably in the wardrobe.' My hand grips the receiver, my knuckles turning white.

'I've looked. It's not there. It's gone.' His voice is a low growl on the other end of the line, grating on my last nerve, and I snap, 'Well, maybe it's in the wash.' Fury overspills as I become more frantic and irritated that he won't get to the point. 'What's going on?'

'You better have washed it.'

I pause for a second, a little stunned, and then erupt. 'Look, I don't care about your shirt.' I push back my chair and stand up, shouting, 'What's happened?' I run my fingers roughly through my hair, trying to process what the hell is going on. 'Why are you calling?'

'No need to shout. I haven't raised my voice at you.' He puts on his extra-calm voice and slowly enunciates each word as if I'm stupid. 'I just need my shirt for tonight, and I don't know where you've put it.'

God, I hate him when he speaks to me in that condescending tone. My chest is tight as I let his words sink in for a moment, the receiver shaking in my hand.

'Let me get this straight – *this* is your emergency?' My blood is boiling, and my voice lowers to a hiss. 'Are you fucking kidding me?'

'What is your problem?'

I truly believe he is oblivious.

'Oh, I haven't seen your dog, by the way.'

My teeth clench in my shaking jaw at his flippancy, and my eyes narrow as I stare at the phone, wanting to smash it to tiny pieces. Every breath is heavy and loud in my ears as I try to calm down enough to respond. 'We've been gone four days and you've only just noticed the dog's not there?' My breathing slows. My shoulders unhunch, and my body starts to feel limp. I am so beyond livid that I am, in fact, calm. I don't have the energy to be angry anymore. I have just given up. Enough is enough.

'So?'

I can't bear to listen to another sickening word. 'We need to talk when I get home.' I calmly hang up and sit back, staring at the phone, speechless, drained.

Diane peeps around the corner before coming into the nook. Without saying a word, she places an ice bucket on the desk with a bottle of whisky and a box of tissues, pats my shoulder, and leaves. I feel too ashamed to make eye contact. Those two lovely women who showed me such concern must have heard everything.

I pour a glass of whisky and take a sip. I shake away the disgusting taste and my eyes water from its strength, but it doesn't matter. I need to drown out his disrespect.

'He didn't even ask after his own daughter,' I say out loud, although no one is there to listen. I am numb, nauseous from the stench of whisky on my breath and the musty smell of old books. I stand for a while as a stream of light highlights the dust in the air, making the quaint little library look hazy and surreal.

I pace back and forth across the small space, brushing my fingers along the woven tapestries covering the wall. I can't do this anymore. I can't keep pretending everything's fine. I have no fight left in me, and I don't think Ben and I have anything left to fight for.

I perch against the dark wooden desk, pushing the phone aside, mindlessly straightening the pile of dusty old books. Am I really prepared for what this means? Do I have the strength to go home and tell Ben? Could I make it alone, just me and Lexi? How would she take it?

I lean back on the table and stare at the mishmash of hanging bulbs and coloured glass shades. It's been so peaceful this week with no arguing. Lexi and I have both been much more relaxed, and my little girl has got her smile back. Maybe she would be able to sleep properly again and be able to concentrate at school? Or would she hate me or go off the rails?

I take a big gulp of whisky and start pacing again. What if Ben wanted custody or made us homeless? I can't imagine he would move out without a huge commotion. But what's a home with no love? What would I be teaching Lexi about relationships and families if I stay?

I stand by the wall, fiddling with the beads dangling from macrame plant hangers. A brass bird cage above them has a sparkly ornamental bird perched on top of the open door. It looks like the bird has escaped its cage – it's free. My heart swells, like I've been gifted with hope.

What if... I could escape my cage too. All I have to do is open the door. 'Are you here to tell me I can do it as well, little bird?' My lips press into a small smile, and I raise my glass to make a toast. 'Thank you. Here's to opening the cage door and flying free.' I take a sip and feel warmth spreading inside my chest.

It may well be the whisky making my imagination soar, but it feels like the bird left me a key inside, ready to open my cage when the time is right.

I stop still at the faint din of applause from the kids' show. I have no idea of the time, but guess the evening entertainment has finished. Guests begin to loudly pour into the hotel and head upstairs to their rooms, children chattering and squealing.

Families laughing and playing together is such a joyful sound. I feel bereft of that joy. I can't steal it from Lexi as well. It's not her fault she's caught in the middle of my problems, and I don't want to ruin her day by being miserable around her. Thankfully, Lexi loves Nanny P putting her to bed, reading stories, singing songs – the happiness I just don't have within me to share right now.

I slump onto the floor cushions, creating a nest of pillows and throws so I can hide from the world. I'll be content with the soft lounge music and gross whisky to keep me company. My eyes wander around the small library nook. It is picture perfect. How I would love to transport it home to have as my own space. If I still have a home.

***

After a short while of deep breaths and even deeper thoughts, a fist appears around the corner of the nook, pretending to rap on the non-existent door.

'Knock knock!'

Startled and gripping the cushion in my lap, I reply, 'Who's there?'

Then two rattling tumblers full of ice appear and out jumps a smiling Prince Charming.

THURSDAY

Let's Be Happy

'*Annyeong!* Mrs Todgers said there was whisky! Let's be happy!'

'Prince Charming?' I laugh in surprise, my chest tightening. My hands spring up to my hair. I must look in a terrible state after the day I've had.

'Off duty. I'm Han Jisung now. How do you do?' He bows and holds out his hand.

'Cally. Pleased to meet you.' I shake his hand, probably for far too long, mesmerised by his dazzling smile. My insides are all of a squiggle.

'Is it OK for me to join you?' His smile is infectious. And a friendly face is just what I need right now.

'Of course!' I nod towards the chair. He takes the bottle from the table, slips off his shoes, and sits next to me in my cushion nest. He hands me a glass and pours a generous double measure, and I fill his glass in return.

'I heard what happened today, with the reporter.' Prince Charming puts his hand to his heart and bows his head. 'I wanted to thank you. I am very grateful.'

'You're welcome. Cheers!' I raise my glass with a smile. The Golden Adonis, Prince Charming, joining me for a drink, is a potent pick-me-up.

'Cheers!' He chinks our glasses together.

'Do I call you Han or...'

'Jisung,' he interrupts, shaking the damp hair that falls soft and fluffy down to his eyes. 'Han is my family name.'

He smells fresh and delicious. Dressed in sweatpants and jumper now that he's finished playing Prince Charming for today, he relaxes back into the cushions, stretching out his long legs.

When he casually drapes an arm along the cushions, my breath catches at the solid muscle behind me. I should move away, create some separation between us. But I can't. I'm in big trouble here. While Jisung looks completely at ease, I have to keep remembering to breathe. I resist the urge to stroke his tight, creamy cashmere jumper. All hopes of not feeling giddy and any lingering playboy misgivings have evaporated. My brain scrabbles around for something interesting to say. I wish I wasn't so tongue-tied around him.

'Had a good day?'

'A great day! Acting, singing, couldn't be better.' His face lights up as he speaks. 'I love this part of the week; the kids are more confident, and they start to shine.'

'Sounds like you really enjoy your job.' I smile.

'It's the best! All fun, no stress. There's never a dull day working with kids. They always make me laugh.'

'How is Lexi getting on?' I ask, missing her cute little face.

'She's really getting into it.' He nods enthusiastically. 'She has a very good voice, good projection and stage presence.' His eyes twinkle. 'Lexi is feisty and cheeky... like her mum.' He grins and fixes his gaze on me, his face warm and oh, so handsome. He angles his body and leans towards me.

'Didn't see you around today?'

'Oh, er, no. I was working.' Attempting to, anyway. I brush my loose hair back behind my ear, my fingers trembling a little from his proximity and attention. I take a large gulp of my drink.

With my temperature rising, I pull my hoodie over my head and feel Jisung tugging the back of my t-shirt down to preserve my modesty. There would have been no coming back from the embarrassment had I accidentally stripped down to my bra.

'Tattoo?'

'Yeah,' I reply, being the dazzling conversationalist that I am.

'May I see?' There is an eagerness in his voice as he leans closer. I lift the back of my t-shirt, purposely this time, to reveal the tattoo in its full glory. A hand-sized hot-air balloon, shaded in sky blue with pink bunting and bows, its black outline beginning to fade and slightly blur with age.

'Wow! It's so detailed and colourful.'

'From my younger days.' I look round to see his eyes shining. 'It's always been top of my bucket list. I love the idea of floating away, rising above it all and escaping.'

'Sounds good. I've never been on a balloon ride. It looks fun to soar through the sky like a bird.' He nods. 'Your tattoo is beautiful.' As he pulls my t-shirt back down, his fingertip lightly brushes my lower back, sending a visible shiver up my spine that makes him quickly pull his hand away.

'I always wanted one, but my work would never allow it.' His voice trails off and he distances himself back against the cushions.

'That's a shame.' He doesn't seem keen to give away any more details.

'Any more tattoos?'

'None I can show in public,' I reply with a cheeky wink. He narrows his eyes.

'You're a secret badass, I'm sure of it.'

I laugh at the suggestion and make a mental note to get a tattoo that can't be shown in public asap.

'What is it you do, Cally?' Jisung grins. 'Now I know you're a journalist but not a journalist.'

'I just write for a parenting magazine.' I shrug and take a smaller sip of my drink. It still burns my throat and makes me shake my head to recover from the taste. 'Kids' stuff, things to do, places to go… it's a mum thing.'

'Ah.' He looks confused. 'Like an influencer?'

'Kind of, but I hide behind my keyboard. I'm not brave enough for videos.'

'Keyboard warrior?'

'No!' I giggle a little too loud, my filters dissolving in alcohol. 'I write nice things. I'm all rainbows and unicorns.' I laugh. 'Coming here is a big deal for me.'

'Yeah,' he says slowly, dipping his head, 'it was a big deal for me too.' He hugs his legs close and stares down at his white socks. I suddenly feel awkward – I don't know him well enough to recognise if I should ask questions or change the subject. And he might not yet trust that I won't write about anything he says. 'We don't have to do an interview this week, if you don't want to.'

He seems to snap out of his thoughts and looks up brightly. 'Thank you, I appreciate that.'

I give a reassuring smile and finish my drink, then use the pause in our conversation as a cue to go to the bathroom.

I stand at the sink with my forehead against the mirror to steady myself. I can't believe today's crazy rollercoaster of emotions is ending by having drinks with Prince Charming! *Me!* My chest is buzzing and I inwardly scream every swear word I can think of. I feel like an infatuated fangirl at a BTS concert. Sorry, Ben who?

I straighten and look into the mirror, my nose scrunching at my reflection. I cover my face with my hands and will myself to be a size zero with immaculate hair and make-up – like the beautiful women he always had an arm around in his photos. But when I open my eyes, I sigh in resignation at the fact I'm still me. Imperfect, plain old me.

I roll my shoulders back and look around for any miracle products, opting for a spray of random perfume from the prettiest bottle. I smooth down the frizz in my hair, ready for a Cally pep talk.

He's just a person. A gorgeous, amazing person, but still just a person. Those women spent hours creating their image. I wish I could have clicked on each photo to see what they looked like before all the apps, filters, Photoshop retouches, and the plastic surgery, botox, lip fillers, fake hair, eyelashes, and shit ton of make-up. I picture the perfect women smiling with grotesque fake teeth and make myself giggle.

Anyway, right now, it's me he's spending time with, not them. This is a one-off chance-in-a-lifetime drink with the most gorgeous man on Earth. I would never forgive myself if I didn't at least *try* to flirt with him. I've got one enchanted evening. What do I have to lose?

The whisky convinces me that flirting is a great idea. I cast my mind back over two decades, trying to remember how to flirt. Hair flick? Is that a thing? I jerk my head back. My feet also stumble backwards, and I have to reach for the sink to keep from falling. So that's a no.

How do people flirt? Maybe I was never a flirter in my youth? Look up through my eyelashes like Princess Di? My eyes flicker upwards. I can't see my eyelashes. I try dipping my head and catch sight of myself in the mirror – I look angry, confused, and cross-eyed. That can't be right.

Do I... twirl my hair? I twiddle my hair around my finger. And now my finger is stuck in a knot. I sigh. This is hard. How about I bite my lip? I look up into the mirror and bite my bottom lip. I look like I'm about to say, *Ohhh, I'm telling my mum.*

I slide my teeth up my lip, not biting so much. My nose scrunches up and I look like a sneering rabbit. Top lip then? That can't be it. My chin and bottom lip jut out, showing a row of bottom teeth, and I look like some kind of Frankenstein.

Fine, no flirting. With a sore lower lip, I take a deep breath, sway a little, and edge out the bathroom door. To my mind, I am sashaying down the corridor back to the nook.

'I thought you'd got lost!' Jisung watches me lower myself into our nest. I sit a bit closer to him than I meant to, but he doesn't move away.

'No, I just had to make sure my mascara was evenly smudged.'

Jisung gazes deeply into my eyes for several heart-stopping seconds, then shakes his head slightly. 'Sorry, I got lost in your eyes for a moment. But yeah, the make-up smudges are a nice touch.'

I playfully swat his arm, laughing. 'How did you say that with a straight face?' A line that corny should not make my heart skip. One point to Team Jisung; my flirting skills could never match this man's natural talents.

'I got lost earlier though!' I squeak. 'I got stuck in that damn maze!'

He laughs. 'Ah yes, the maze. I got lost too when I first came here.'

'I'm glad it's not just me.'

Jisung rearranges the cushions in our nest and thoughtfully places one behind my back. 'So, you're a writer – what's the dream? Books? Plays?'

'You know, I've always wanted to write children's books.' His eyes are focused intently on me, like he's interested in what I have to say. 'No one's ever asked about my writing aspirations before.' It's... strange, but makes me feel... acceptable? Important, even?

'You should go for it!' He smiles. 'I'll buy your first book and you can autograph it for me.'

The thought makes me giggle. 'How about you? Broadway? Hollywood?'

'I don't know. Do you think I would make a good action hero?' He smirks, puffs up his chest, and poses, flexing all his muscles.

I squeeze his bicep and do a Lexi-style dramatic faint. Despite my goofy grin, can he tell my swoon is *very* real?

'Maybe I could be the first Korean Bond. What do you think?' He twists his body towards me and strikes a model pose, eyebrow raised, lips pouting. Just wow. I fan my face with my hand, pretending I'm acting. He is H. O. T. He laughs and poses with a wink and his widest smile, pointing at his cute dimple. 'Good-looking, huh?'

I giggle. 'Oh, are you? I hadn't noticed.' He laughs and makes an exaggerated effort to flatten his hair into a silly middle parting.

'Do you ever have a bad hair day like us normal people?'

'Hey, I'm normal!' He laughs and ruffles his funny hairstyle. 'You should see me when I wake up, hair sticking out everywhere!'

Oh my goodness, yes please. I'd love to wake up next to you and, err, see your hair. He reaches out to stroke my curls. 'You are lucky. You have naturally beautiful hair.'

I fiddle with the hem of my trousers, not knowing how to respond.

'Ahh, you are shy with compliments. That's cute.'

'Ahem. Let's change the topic.' Before I spontaneously combust. 'Do you have a nickname?'

'G. Just the letter, like *Ji*sung. What about you?'

'Ha! Dilly-dally, because I'm always late. Not on purpose, I just... can't help it.' I snigger. 'Your question.'

'Sunrise or sunset, Dilly-Dally?'

Even that silly old tease sounds sensual in his velvet baritone. 'Sunrise. The start of a wonderful new day. Not that I ever see it! You?'

'Same, and same reason. Your question.'

'Do you sleep with your socks on, G?' I ask.

'Of course not! You don't, do you?'

'No.' I laugh at how outraged he is by the idea.

A mischievous grin spreads over his face. 'My question. In bed... big spoon or little spoon?'

My cheeks heat at the picture that pops in my head. He's learned exactly how to make me squirm. 'I think I'm probably a little spoon. You?' Why does this feel so intimate? It's like we're speed dating. Not that I've ever been speed dating, or any kind of dating for... too many years to count. I need to drink more.

'Big spoon.' He flexes his muscles again. I swoon. 'Your question.'

I'm sure he enjoys making me blush. I better move away from bedroom thoughts. 'Do you believe in parallel universes?'

131

'Yeah, sure. Why not? You?'

'Same. Your turn.'

'What's the most romantic thing someone could do for you?'

Damn that mischievous look in his eyes. More drink. 'I don't know, pass. Next question.' It's been far too long to remember romance.

'No, no passes... Flowers? Chocolates? Cooking you a special meal?' He brings his fingers to his lips to add a chef's kiss, making it even harder to think of an answer.

'OK, erm... a cuddle on the couch and asking me how my day was.'

He puts down his glass and settles his eyes on me with curiosity. 'That's it? No expensive restaurants? No gifts?'

'Nope.'

He shakes his head. 'Wow, that's refreshing.'

'Hmm?'

'The women I meet in my industry are very high maintenance. They always want expensive things. I could never tell if they liked me for me, or just what they wanted from me.'

'I can't believe anyone would like money or things more than you! Have you never met you?'

He cocks his head to the side and looks at me for a moment, as if he's working out if I'm joking.

It seems Jisung isn't quite as self-assured as Prince Charming. It's a relief to find some dents in his perfection. There's a vulnerability about him, no ego or narcissism. Which makes him even more charming and... perfect. How does he do that? How does he turn an imperfection into a perfection? And yet he doesn't seem to see it.

'They just weren't the right women for you,' I say in my most genuine and consoling voice. He nods and studies my face for a long moment, a smile slowly spreading its warmth. 'And all you want is a cuddle?'

'I'd just like a little bit of time and affection. And you?'

'Ah... I would like a surprise. Something small and thoughtful.'

This man! He's not just a pretty face. He's so down-to-earth. Ugh!

'Oh, my question. What do you do to unwind?' Did that sound suggestive? His eyes have narrowed like he's thinking impure thoughts.

'Let's say, swimming.' He smirks. 'You?'

'Sleep. I never really unwind – I'm busy or I'm asleep. Your question.'

'Do you believe in love at first sight?'

I feel called out. He can't know, surely? Not that I'm in love or anything.

'Yes. You?'

'Same. Your question.'

I will not over-think. I will focus. I will drink a bit more.

'Where would you like your forever home?' I ask.

'Anywhere I'm happy. You?'

'Here in Fairy-Tale Wonderland, in a little mushroom house deep in the woods for me and Lexi, away from all the noise and busyness.'

'Ha! Yes, I like that idea. We could grow our own vegetables.'

'And bake cakes.'

Jisung's face lights up. 'And have campfires.'

'And toast marshmallows.'

'And hear the pitter patter of lots of puppy paws.'

'Awww, yes. And spend the evenings reading.'

'And have late-night chats.'

Could this man be any more perfect? My hand is on my chest, loving every second of this shared dream. 'Looking up at the stars.'

'And go on midnight adventures.'

'And then have breakfast in bed.'

'And swim in the river.'

'Maybe add in a couple of unicorns too. Ahhh, sounds perfect!' I sigh wistfully. We smile at each other, like we're both enjoying the wonderful thought bubble we've created together. He's in the scene I imagine. Am I in his? 'Your question.'

A smile flickers on his lips. 'What would be your ideal date?'

'It would be...' It's been so long since I've been on a date. 'Erm... a walk. Taking Barney, our dog, for a walk in the woods by a stream on a warm summer's evening.'

'Really? You can choose anything!' He sounds amused, his face crinkling in confusion. 'No helicopter? Casino? Michelin stars? Yacht?'

'I would be a cheap date.' I shrug my shoulders and laugh. 'Maybe stopping for an ice cream. Just lovely company and conversation is all I would like. You?'

'I was going to say a walk along an empty beach at sunset, but now it sounds like I'm copying! But I'm going to add a blanket, some champagne, and some sexy time.' He wiggles his eyebrows at me and laughs. I laugh and push away the images in my mind.

'Your question,' he says, still grinning.

'Favourite colour?'

'Grey – like your eyes. You?'

I'm thrown that he's noticed my eyes. 'Err... red, like...' I want to say his lips.

'Your cheeks when I make you blush.'

Argh! I can feel my cheeks burning brighter. I hide them behind my hands.

'So cute.' He smiles. 'OK, sorry, you can have a free go – what's something you like about me that will make me blush?'

'Just one thing? How do I choose? Hmm... your dimples when you smile.'

He pretends to giggle and hide his blushes. But I'm sure his ears turn a little pink.

'You can have a proper turn.' He pretends to still be hiding behind a cushion.

'How are you single? Do you want to get married? Have a family?'

'Is that a proposal? You want to marry me?' Jisung laughs, and his laugh deepens when I try to hide my red cheeks behind my cushion.

'Yes, I'd like to get married. I suppose I don't need to ask you?'

'Well, no.' I sigh. 'But I would like to be *happily* married and have a *happy* family.'

Oops. Until now, our chatting has been frivolous and fun, avoiding anything *heavy*. He's too easy to talk to. I hope I haven't ruined the atmosphere. Jisung throws his hands up in the air, making me jump. His brows pinch together, his smile disappears, and he lays his hand on mine. I flinch and stare wide-eyed, waiting for him to speak.

'Cally, I've been meaning to ask you something,' he begins, his voice low and serious. 'Do... you... like cheese?'

We both erupt in laughter and I launch myself at him, slapping and tickling whichever body parts I can reach. Before I know it, we're in a full-scale tickle fight. Legs, arms, and cushions are flying. He's just as ticklish as me and we roll around on the floor, both laughing hysterically. After a few minutes of tickle torture, he rolls me onto my back, kneels over me, and pins my arms to the floor. I squirm to free myself, but I'm powerless against those muscles. He holds me there, both of us giggling while we catch our breath.

He must be able to feel the pulse in my wrists going berserk. His eyes are still smiling, locked onto mine. I swallow down my sudden nerves. We're still playing, right? Then in one swift move, he pulls me up and positions me back against the cushions.

'Phwooo!' I grab a book and fan my face. 'That's the hottest thing that's happened to me in years!' Damn you, whisky, for removing my inhibitions. I smack my hand over my mouth, but my hands are drunk and I hit the book into my face instead. We both burst out laughing. I cover my eyes, not daring to make eye contact.

When we can eventually sit quietly again, Jisung refills our glasses. 'What about... the place you would most like to be kissed?'

'Is this the whisky asking now?'

'Ha, maybe a little.'

I giggle. 'I'd like a steamy kiss up against a tree. You?'

'You've thought about that before! You had that answer ready!'

'Ha, yeah! My secret's out! Your turn to answer.'

He smirks. 'I was going to say inner thigh.'

'Mr G, you are a very cheeky man!' I chuck a cushion at him.

'But you like it, yeah?' He wiggles his eyebrows again, making us both laugh. Oh yes, I like it. Very much indeed.

'Your question.'

Extremely distracted by the thought of thigh kisses, it takes me a moment to think. 'OK, place you would *not* like to be kissed?'

'Hmm...' He looks up and down his body. I happily copy. 'The only place would be my feet.'

'Ewww! Who kisses feet? Mine would be belly button. Way too tickly.'

'Aww no?' He reaches out towards my stomach and then snatches his hands back. 'That's ruined all the fun I had planned.'

We laugh again, and I throw another cushion at him.

'Talking of bellies, have you eaten?' he asks, still sniggering.

'I can't remember eating at all today.'

'Let's go.'

We take the final sips from our glasses; then Jisung pulls me to my feet, catching me as I sway. Stumbling and giggling, we each loudly hush the other, which makes us giggle even more.

We stagger arm in arm, zig-zagging through the leafy conservatory, holding each other upright. Although, there is a tiny possibility that it's mostly me who's staggering and he's trying to hold me up.

As we approach the exit, I remember to sashay. Unfortunately, I swing my hip a little too forcefully, struggle to keep my balance, and trip over my own foot. As I slip out of Jisung's arm and tumble in slow motion towards the ground, he catches me before I faceplant, holding me steady until I find my footing.

It's then that we both look down.

His face turns to sheer horror as he realises one hand has grabbed my arm, but the other is on my boob. He whisks his hands away, saying, 'I'm sorry! I'm so sorry!' over and over as we blunder out of the door. We make it outside and I am stuck to the spot, bent double, giggling uncontrollably. He stands with his hand over his face. Every time I think I can hold it together, I look up, see how mortified he is, and the laughter starts all over again.

Eventually, my giggles die out enough for us to continue on our food mission. The alcohol effects hit harder in the fresh air, and he puts his arm around my waist to help me walk in a straight line. I leave the swagger for another time.

We walk all the way around the kitchens to a cosy seating area dimly glowing in candlelight – a small three-sided patio with plush pink furniture. I sit on the closest, most inviting sofa while Prince Charming switches on the patio heaters and takes a furry cream throw out of the ottoman opposite. He walks around the central wooden table and gently covers me with the blanket. I pull it up to my chin and stroke the warm fur over my cheeks.

'I'll get us something to eat. What would you like?'

'But it's late. Won't they be closed?'

'The kitchens are always open. Lots of staff work through the night – caterers, cleaners, maintenance, even the gardeners.'

'Cool!' I light up at the prospect of food. I'm ravenous. 'Please could I have some fries?'

'Coming right up. I'll be back in a minute. Will you be OK here?'

I smile and nod. As he walks away, I kick my feet and throw my head back, singing out, 'Swoooooon!' to the night's sky.

Whoops, I hope he didn't hear that. But he is lush! I hope I'm making a better impression. At least it wasn't me who embarrassed themselves this time. He touched my boob, ha!

I snuggle under the blanket and admire my new outdoor nest. Two walls are grass, and the one behind is brick with climbing vines and little pink flowers that create a small canopy overhead. I study the flickering candles of the gold candelabra on the table, never quite sure what is real and what is artificial and childproof.

So... if we got married... would I become Han Cally Jackson? No, Han Jackson Cally? Oh. Wait. Will I stay as Jackson now or go back to my maiden name? But that would mean me and Lexi would have different surnames.

Jisung is back in a flash, carrying a tray of goodies that he places on the low table.

'Come under.' I pull back the throw and shuffle closer to him to cover us both. He hands me a plate of yummy thick chips with a big squirt of ketchup on one side and a blob of mayonnaise on the other. I squeal in appreciation.

'I didn't know which you prefer.' He offers me a bottle. 'Beer?'

'No, thank you. I think I might be a tiddly bit drunk already.'

He opens a bottle for himself and relaxes back, holding a steaming bowl. I peer over. 'Ooh! What's that?'

'Want to try?'

He calls it something I might struggle to pronounce even when sober and holds out his chopsticks. I lean in, and he feeds me a mouthful of noodles. I slurp and splash sauce on my face before swallowing. My tongue is on *FIRE!* My eyes water, my nose runs, and my tongue hangs out of my mouth like a dog's while I flap my hands trying to cool it down. I reach out and grab the beer from Prince Charming's hand and glug until the burning eases. He watches me, open-mouthed and highly amused.

'It's not even spicy!' He crinkles his nose and laughs, putting his hand on my shoulder. 'Shall I get you some milk?'

'No, I'm fine, but thanks for offering.' Even with my mouth on fire, I know I would do it again to see another one of his gorgeous smiles. 'Chip?'

He opens his mouth and I pop one in.

'I'm sorry I was rude when we met.' Jisung bows his head towards me. 'You did nothing wrong. I've had a bad time with reporters.' A huge smile spreads across my face. So it was never about me! Or chocolate smudges! Or cheese! It was the job he thought I did. His apology warms me to the tips of my toes.

'That's OK. You did save my life, and you're lovely now.' I wink. In my alcohol-fuelled state, it is actually more of a double-eyed wink.

I quickly finish my chips and sit back, patting my full stomach. I try not to make it obvious that I'm watching him still eat, but I can't tear my eyes away. And the appreciative noises he makes with each mouthful give me tingles in body parts I'd forgotten exist. He takes my plate and puts it on the table. 'It's good when people enjoy their food.' He smiles, taking a napkin and wiping the sauce from my chin. 'I like women who are curvy and juicy.'

I giggle at his choice of words, but with his face full of mischief, I think he actually means them.

I can't wipe the silly grin from my face. The chips were perfect. In fact, the whole evening has been perfect and I don't want it to end. This wonderful man has been the tonic I needed. And even if he is sleeping with Cinderella, well, she's not here now. And the number of women he's dated before hasn't made the slightest difference. And... none of the women in the photos were curvy.

'Mmm, that was good.' He nods, wiping his mouth. He rests back on the couch, turning his head and smiling back at me.

'Thank you for this evening.' I try not to sound as soppy as I feel. 'It was a rough day.' He gives me a playful nudge in the arm, and I nudge him back. It was only a small elbow movement, but it felt pretty deep and meaningful.

I yawn and wriggle up close to Jisung, kicking off a shoe and curling my leg beneath me on the sofa. I rest my head on his broad shoulder and look up at his square jawline, admiring his perfect skin and cute little ears, gazing up to his tousled hair that looks so soft.

'Mmmm... How are you so... perfect?'

'What's priceless to one is worthless to another.'

'What? Who would... could ever think *you* were worthless?' I wave my hand dismissively under the throw. 'You're charming and funny and kind and talented and confident and fit and calm, and you're comfy and warm and I don't want you to move.' I snuggle closer into his neck. 'Please will you tell me a story in Korean?'

His smooth, rhythmic tones wash over me like waves of comfort and lull me into a state of total relaxation. My eyelids flutter and, in time, close.

I drift in and out of consciousness, imagining that I'm flying. One minute I'm having a piggyback ride and passing the library nook. Next, I'm floating upwards, snuggling into the softest bear with its big arms around me. Then I sense the whole world turning upside down and I float along the upside-down corridor until I'm on my feet, fumbling for my room key. Then I'm lying in bed and I see Nanny P watching over me. Prince Charming is at my bedside, and when he leans over and strokes my hair, I know I must be dreaming.

FRIDAY

Spillage

'**M**um! Get up!'

'Ugh.' My head is pounding. 'Water,' I rasp, shielding my eyes from daylight and the spinning room. 'Please, Lexi.'

'Come on, Mum, I'm starving,' she whines, pulling the covers off my bed.

'Uggghh!'

'Why are you dressed already?'

I half open one eye and peer down. Yep, fully dressed in the clothes from last night, but with just one shoe on. I don't remember going to bed. I remember the corridor was upside down. Ugghhh, it makes no sense.

'Muu-uum!'

'All right, all right, I'm coming.' I haul myself out of bed, catching sight of a bedraggled mess in the mirror. Lexi tugs at my arm.

'Shower later. You look fine,' she clearly lies. I attempt to smooth down my scarecrow hair, looking around for my other shoe.

'Mum!'

I abandon the search, slip on a pair of trainers, and try to catch up as Lexi flies out of the door.

'What's the rush?'

'Mum! It's breakfast with the three bears, remember?'

I don't remember. My head hurts. *Right, come on, Cally, you can do this. Just act like everything's normal.* I wipe the sleepy dust from my eyes and lick my finger to wipe away the remnants of yesterday's smudge of mascara.

As we pass the reception desk, Diane looks at me pityingly and discreetly passes my missing shoe with a knowing nod. Right now, I feel too trashed to wonder what she knows.

The Al Fresco Bears Breakfast is a non-hangover-friendly riot of noise and excited children. Lexi runs off to join in the fun and games with the bear characters, leaving me to nurse my poor head with an extremely strong coffee. I flop onto a seat, close my eyes, and let the fresh breeze blow away the cobwebs.

'Good morning,' comes a singsong voice at my table. Mrs Life-and-Soul. I manage to lift my head enough to smile weakly.

'You look like you need this.' She speaks with a softer voice that doesn't hurt my ears while placing a plate of cleverly sliced fruit salad arranged like a bear's face in front of me. Then, with a cheeky wink, a glass of what I now recognise to be whisky.

'Vitamins and hair of the dog,' she announces and, with a friendly chuckle, returns to the party. Nausea strikes as the pungent smell wafts up my nose, but if it makes me feel human again, I'll try anything. I down the whisky, shake my head at the revolting taste, and wash it down with coffee.

I slowly pick at the fruit and reconsider Mrs Life-and-Soul. Maybe she's not so bad after all, just a bit louder than I'm used to. I've been so caught up in my own thoughts that I've not been very friendly at all. I wouldn't have noticed if she was hungover; I don't even know her real name.

Determined not to analyse the repercussions of yesterday's events, somehow I do remember my appointment to interview the resort manager this afternoon. Ugh. Great timing. As I'm about to casually lay my head on the table, a little hand pulls at my elbow.

'Mum! The bears said all parents have to join in – no excuses.'

In my weak and feeble state, I am unwillingly dragged to the bears' dancefloor.

The hours go past in a blur of balloons, dance routines, songs, and games. And face paints. And although I've been in hangover hell, it's actually been great fun, and Lexi looked thrilled that I joined in with her. Fuelled by Lexi's smiles and the coffee on tap, I even manage to survive past the bears' lunchtime barbecue before I'm ready to collapse. I could kiss Nanny P when she arrives with fresh energy to take over.

I collect my shoe and find Lexi to tell her I need to go. She's mid-dance routine and barely acknowledges I've said goodbye. I try not to feel put out, remembering a time I couldn't even go to the bathroom without her holding my hand. But here, she has the opportunity to gain some independence, and I'm so proud to see how my little girl is growing into a confident young lady.

I slope off to the quiet courtyard for a fix of nicotine, hoping that will help me feel like a functioning person again. When I'm through the private door and on the path to the courtyard, I hear voices inside and stop. I want as few people as possible to see me in this state (and with my face painted as a clown). But the woman's voice is raised and angry, and I can't help but wonder what's going on.

I creep to the end of the path and peek around the corner. Cinderella and Prince Charming. Again. I dart back against the wall, my heart hammering. What on earth is going on? Why is she shouting?

'You can't take time off. You are here to be on my arm.'

I'm shocked that her harsh tones are nothing like the sweet, mild-mannered girl I met before. So she really did put on an act during our interview. I can't hear Jisung reply, only my heartbeat thumping in my ears.

'Say something!' she screams. 'Guests will complain if Prince Charming isn't there to marry me. That's the role of a *supporting cast member*, to *support* the star of the show!'

I blink each time she snaps her fingers to emphasise a word.

'There may be casting agents here. You need to be on stage to make me shine.'

This is no lovers' tiff. There is no love here, let alone professionalism or respect.

I want to shout to Jisung and tell him to put her back in her place. How dare she speak to him like that? I risk another peek to check he's OK. He's just sitting there, head down, fiddling with his ring. Stand up for yourself!

I can't listen to any more in case I step in, and I don't want Jisung to know I'm eavesdropping. I backtrack to my room without any nicotine, and without a clue why he let her say those things.

This shower has a big task ahead. It needs to wash away a hangover and cleanse my thoughts of... everything, so I can focus on work.

**

An essential nap and a shower later, I am revitalised and waiting for Mr Todgers at reception. I am even slightly early, which, in the long history of Cally, is unheard of!

The minutes tick by on the big old grandfather clock. Being kept waiting is really annoying. I can see why people often seem cross when I eventually arrive anywhere.

From behind the reception desk, Diane keeps apologising on behalf of her very busy husband, telling me she's sure he won't be long. She's kind. Even though she's rushing around, she keeps making time to check in and speak to me. She chats briefly about this and that – asking about Lexi, about my work, about my lovely Barney dog.

I keep shifting my weight from one foot to the other and have to stop my foot tapping along with the clock's second hand. After thirty-seven minutes, just as I think I've been forgotten, Mr Todgers breezes through the door.

'Cathy! So pleased you could make it.' The stench of stale cigar smoke and liquor drifts in with him. His cheeks are ruddy, and he stretches out his arms to greet me.

'It's Cally, my love,' Diane whispers through gritted teeth.

'Cally, of course, that's what I said.' Ah, good old Mr Todgers. With his powerful presence, he reminds me of a school headmaster – never in the wrong, and can switch on the charm on demand.

'*Cally,*' he emphasises slowly, 'have they kept you fed and watered?'

I can't resist replying with a playful 'woof' while flashing a sweet smile. For a split second, he furrows his brow, obviously wondering if he heard correctly, then blinking the thought away. Out of the corner of my eye, I see Diane laughing silently behind her husband's back.

He puts his arm around my shoulder, turning me towards the door, saying, 'Walk with me.' I hurry through the door before him, freeing myself from his arm. 'Let's show you some places you haven't discovered yet.'

'I found the maze yesterday.' I hope he's not planning to take me back to that awful place.

'Oh yeah, that was my idea.' He puffs up his chest, very proud of himself. 'Fun, isn't it?'

I don't think he'd appreciate my opinion, so I don't reply. He doesn't notice.

Crunching along the gravel path, we pass the garden where the children are rehearsing for tomorrow's show. I duck behind a row of tall orange blooms in case I exist in front of Lexi's new friends and embarrass her. And in case Prince Charming should look over. I can already feel my cheeks burning. Memories of drunken antics hit differently in daylight, especially when I must have passed out and don't remember getting to bed.

'You've met our fantastic cast?' Mr Todgers points over to the kids' activities. 'All professionals, even an international superstar,' he boasts. 'And, of course, my niece, a real star in my eyes.'

'Oh! Which character is she?'

'Cinderella. She's a beauty, isn't she?'

'She is,' I agree as things begin to fall into place. Uncle's star of the show. Even as her boss, Jisung must worry he'd risk his job by standing up to her.

'Yeah, beautiful, but a pain in the ass.' He shakes his head. I stifle a snort.

We follow the path past the pool. I look on in envy at the guests lying peacefully in the warm sunshine, enjoying their time off work. Then I remember this is the person who paid for our trip here, so I give him my full attention and take my turn at being schmoozed.

'We have characters and settings the kids recognise, but our storylines are fluid. The cast improvise depending on what the kids wish for.'

I'm sure I read parts of what he said in the resort brochure. He must say the same thing every time he shows someone around.

We amble past the Secret Garden at Mr Todgers' relaxed pace and come to a vast vegetable garden. He waves his arm towards the impressive plot. 'We grow as much fresh produce as we can on-site.'

'Incredible! I had no idea this place existed!' We continue walking past rows upon rows of ripening fruits and vegetables. It's yet another part of the resort I would love a photo of.

'Could I just quickly ask about the no cameras or phones policy?'

He notices I try to subtly ensure the phone in my bag is switched off.

'Don't worry.' He gives a dismissive flick of his hand. 'It's fine for staff. We just remind everyone to keep it low key.

'We want our guests to have an escape from reality, to be fully present here with their kids, and to play together as a family. We saw parents were still working on their phones or engrossed in taking photos of their kids having fun, but not being part of that fun – especially mothers. One day, kids will look back on their childhood photos and wonder why their mom isn't in any of them.'

I think about our family photos, and he's right; I'm not in many. Ben has never been one to take photos, and I'm not one for selfies.

'We have professional photographers at the resort to take action shots of our guests having fun together. We don't want forced smiles and poses; we want fun and magic to be etched into our guests' memories. Then we give each family a photo book of their holiday with us.'

I nod along enthusiastically, impressed by the depth of insight and wisdom in his words, seeing the brilliance in what had seemed like a crazy rule only moments before.

'That makes so much sense now. It's a great idea. I've enjoyed seeing my daughter not constantly on her tablet.'

'Is she having fun?' He takes a quick break from his sales pitch.

'Absolutely. Neither of us wants to leave.'

He beams proudly. 'That's what I like to hear.'

Mr Todgers reaches over the fence to pick a juicy, ripe cherry tomato and tosses it to me. I pop it in my mouth, surprised I even managed to catch it, and try not to squirt the pips down my front.

'We pick our marketing photos to show just a few highlights of our resort, but we want to keep secrets for our guests to discover for themselves once they're here. We have new secrets each season. You should see this place in winter.'

'Oh, I'd love to. I bet it's a magical winter wonderland.' I'm sold. I can just imagine how magnificent it must be with all the resort's resources – ice castles and snow queens and sleigh rides.

He laughs and holds a branch away for me to pass. 'Better start saving!'

Ouch. Way to destroy a dream with three little words.

Next on the tour are fields full of flowers on each side of the path. 'Wow!' I lean closer to one of the clumps of bright yellow flowers. 'We're in flower heaven!' I inhale deeply. 'Mmm. I've never seen anything like this.' Flowers of all kinds sectioned by colour, rose bushes in coloured rows like straight rainbows, lavender as far as the eye can see, and a field of pastel confetti. I slowly turn around, taking in the full panorama. 'It's breathtaking.'

I gasp, hand on my chest. I'm schmoozed. Mr Todgers glows like I've given him a personal compliment. The resort is obviously an extension of him, a culmination of his life's work. It's incredible, and he knows it.

'You've probably noticed we get through a lot of flowers to decorate the resort.'

'It always looks remarkable.'

'We have a talented team of floral designers.'

'I've seen the catering ninj... err... staff setting up – very impressive. You must employ a lot of staff.'

'Yeah, we have a large staff accommodation village. We're fortunate to have high staff retention.'

'So much thought has gone into the resort. Where did the idea come from?' I ask, trailing my hands through the flowers.

'We created the resort for our beautiful daughter, Lottie. She loved fairy tales and had a vivid imagination, pretending to experience all the magical places she dreamed of.'

'Awww, you made her dreams come true. She must love it here?'

Mr Todgers dips his head and clears his throat. 'Sadly, she's no longer with us.'

My mouth drops, and I'm choked for words. I feel absolutely awful for asking the question.

'She used to beg me to join in with her fantasy games, but I was always too busy...' He trails off and looks away. 'After we lost Lottie, I regretted every wasted moment, every time I refused her pleas to play.'

'Oh my goodness,' I whisper, my fist squeezed over my heart. 'I'm so sorry. I had no idea.' His revelation shakes me to my core.

'Thank you.' He nods slowly. 'I created this fantasy land so families could enjoy those precious moments together, creating magical memories for the kids, of course, but also for the parents.' I blink back the tears welling in my eyes and feel immense admiration for his vision. And I see him in a new light – as a heartbroken dad.

We walk in silence until the end of the flower fields, where we reach an archway through a high stone wall with a closed black metal gate. As Mr Todgers unlocks the gate, he tells me, 'This is Lottie's private memorial garden.' He gestures for me to enter first.

'You're one of the privileged few who get to come inside.'

'I'm very grateful. Thank you.'

I gasp as I step into the garden and my hand flies to my heart, overwhelmed by both its love and emptiness. A statue of a little girl cuddling a teddy bear is the focal point, surrounded by a bed of white lilies and faced by a solitary bench. White roses climb the walls of the small, enclosed space, and the ground is laid to lawn. The atmosphere is meditative and serene. And sad.

'Is this Lottie?' I ask gently.

'This is my Lottie with her favourite bear.' His voice is full of sorrow; it's hard to hear.

'She's beautiful.' I feel so terribly sorry for him and his lovely wife. 'The garden is a beautiful tribute.'

Mr Todgers lifts his head and gives a small smile. 'Thank you.' He walks to the statue and appears to say a quiet prayer. When he turns back, he says, 'Come, let's finish our chat in the lounge. My treat.'

We exit the garden, Mr Todgers locks the gate, and we retrace our steps to the hotel in a more sombre mood.

I give him some quiet time with his thoughts before I speak. 'Thank you for your time, Mr Todgers. May I ask what made you choose *me* to review the resort?'

'We wanted someone who had never experienced luxury or an exclusive resort, someone who would be awed by their once-in-a-lifetime holiday and tell their people how all their dreams came true here.'

I'm sure by 'my people' he meant my readers, but it felt as if he meant poor people like me, who would have to save up forever to come here. He was so sensitive and sentimental just moments ago, then seemed to go from grieving father back to pompous headmaster. I suppose it must be difficult to transition back into work mode after being in the memorial garden. I'm sure he wasn't being patronising. I must have got the wrong impression.

***

We stand at the bar, the lounge heaving with guests behind us. In the daytime, it's a warm and inviting area, with families relaxing over afternoon tea. But as evening descends, it takes on an air of swanky sophistication. The men have swapped their shorts for high-end suits, while the women sip cocktails in their designer dresses.

Mr Todgers was right; I'm not like these paying guests. My body shrinks lower as I feel conspicuously underdressed – even though jeans and t-shirt are a step up from my usual work-at-home pyjamas. I'm an outsider looking in at this different world. And here I am, having a drink with the owner. I am so far from my comfort zone, whereas Mr Todgers looks like he's back in his natural habitat.

He sits on a barstool and asks the bartender for two bottles of the finest, then turns to me and winks. 'One each.' My stomach churns. I hope he doesn't expect me to spend all evening with him. He pours us each a glass of *the finest*. I don't know the etiquette rules at this social level, and, feeling uncomfortable, down mine in one go.

He refills my glass without hesitation and lights up a cigar indoors – isn't that illegal nowadays?

'So you like my place, then?' Waving a glass in one hand, cigar in the other, he gives off gangster vibes. Or conman with a touch of sleaze, anyway.

'It's very impressive. I feel extremely lucky and grateful to be here.'

'Good, good.' He smirks.

A tall, lanky man slaps Mr Todgers on the back. 'How are you doing, old chap?' Mr Todgers slips off his stool to loudly greet him with even more back slapping. He waves his hand towards me. 'Cathy Jackson, our visiting journalist. Not quite the Pulitzer Prize winner we wanted.' He laughs heartily at me. Mr Lanky laughs louder. I'm not sure if my polite smile shows through my scowl as Todgers introduces Mr Lanky-and-Equally-Pompous. Todgers turns his back to me for their loud Old Boys' Club chat, flashing their expensive watches at each other like peacocks.

Thanks, gods of happy hour. Not fitting in wasn't enough anxiety, obviously. Had to throw in a bit of looking foolish. The bar snacks help, but still, not only do *I* worry my review won't be good enough, but Todgers doesn't think I can do it either. Well, I'll show him. Maybe. And now I have to stand here alone and ignored.

The sound of someone clearing their throat in my ear makes me jump and spin around. An elegant older woman with fierce eyebrows pencilled onto her pinched face stands there flaunting her affluence with diamonds. Clicking her fingers in my face. I jerk my head back, trapped against the bar. The woman's sharp green eyes look me up and down with disapproval. She scoffs in disgust and points to a table. 'Spillage.'

Despite being startled by her rudeness, I reach for a bar mat and hold it out to her. The woman gasps, her hand flying to her chest. 'The audacity! I don't clean! Go and do it!' She gets louder and more incredulous with each word. Her reaction is so ridiculous, it's almost laughable. 'Sorry, I don't work here,' I manage to reply politely.

Before I can turn away, she's shouting in my face. 'I can see you're not doing any work; you're leaving customers waiting. And how disgusting to take a break where guests can see you.'

My jaw tenses at her outburst, and as I wipe her spittle from my cheek, indignation smoulders within me. How dare she be so rude to me, or anyone? Is this what the staff have to put up with? I don't want to cause any more of a scene, but I have to shut this nonsense down and stand up for myself. 'Firstly, I don't appreciate being spoken to like that, and secondly, I'm just a journalist.'

The woman's eyes grow wide before she screeches, 'How dare you talk back to me? I don't care what character you play. Clean my table!' She grabs my elbow, catching me off guard. As my arm jerks, drink sloshes out of the glass I'm still holding.

Grasping at her pristine leopard print dress, the woman lets out a piercing shriek. 'My dress! It's ruined! You'll pay for this, you stupid girl. I'll have you fired.' My heart drops to the floor. I'm stunned, speechless. I stare in disbelief, unable to see any sign of damage. As far as I could see, my drink splashed on the floor.

The lounge goes deadly silent, and all the guests watch as the woman takes my arm in a vice grip and drags me towards her table. Without time to feel mortified, I almost fall flat on my face as I'm thrown off balance. The glass slips from my hand, smashing to smithereens, and I knock a barstool banging to the ground as I stumble. I shout, 'Get your hands off me.' But my voice is drowned out by her screaming, 'Give me your name. I'm speaking to your manager. You won't get away with this.'

When she deposits me at her table, she plants her hands on her hips, screaming, 'Clean it!'

It takes a moment for me to find my feet. I stand up straight, look her in the eye, and firmly state, 'My name is Cally Jackson. I am a journalist.'

She ignores me while she scans her dress and points to the place it's supposedly ruined. 'This cost more than you'll ever earn, and it's ruined! My holiday is ruined!'

I look back at the bar, hoping for some assistance from Todgers. But instead, I find him and his buddy watching and laughing. He throws a piece of popcorn in the air, catching it in his mouth with a smirk. I'm so outraged by the sight of him enjoying my humiliation, I struggle to hold back the urge to vomit.

The woman's sneering voice pierces through my thoughts, demanding my attention once again. 'And you still haven't cleaned my table!'

I fold my arms across my chest to hide that my hands are shaking as rage courses through my veins. 'You're really getting on my tits now,' I shout louder than intended. 'Why don't you try cleaning up your own bloody mess like the rest of us do?'

At that moment, a greying clump of hair I would recognise anywhere bobs to the woman's side. Mrs Life-and-Soul nudges the woman, who falls back into her seat. 'Sit down, you silly woman. You're making a show of yourself.'

I snort-laugh at the bizarre unfolding of events. The woman's mouth hangs open, and she's flabbergasted as she looks back and forth between the two of us. She flicks her thinning fringe to each side and then holds out her palm towards Todgers. 'Finally!'

I scowl at Todgers as he saunters over with a cloth. 'Aren't you going to say something?'

'My apologies, ma'am. I'll clean up for you.' He wipes the table while the woman acts the victim.

'This impertinent girl is insufferable. I want her fired, now!'

'Absolutely, ma'am, fired with immediate effect,' Todgers replies, his tone dripping with sarcasm. 'We just can't get the staff these days.' He sighs and pats the air to shush me.

Rage boils within me, bursting forth as I pound my fist on the table. 'What? I don't even work here! I'm a journalist!'

Just as I could slap the amusement from Todgers' face, I'm interrupted by a familiar voice beside me. 'Sorry I'm late.'

With a warm arm around my shoulders, the tall man at my side guides me away from the creep in front of me. 'Ms Jackson, shall we do my interview now?' I look up to see the calm, smiling face of Jisung. 'I've got you,' he whispers. I breathe a sigh of relief, grateful for his timing.

I am literally a damsel in distress being rescued by Prince Charming. Well, more a wild, raging woman about to be arrested, ruin her career, and be escorted from the resort, but still. He just swooped in from out of nowhere, like a guardian angel. I am totally smitten.

The woman shrieks, 'What? What interview? Where do you think you're going? What about my dress?'

Mrs Life-and-Soul reaches to pat my arm and nods. 'You go, my love. I saw the whole thing. Leave this with me.'

I give her a weary smile and mouth a thank you. But I'm still furious and breathing hard. I step away from Jisung for a quick moment, leaving Mrs Life-and-Soul batting her eyelashes at him, and stride back to the bar. I step around the barman clearing the broken glass and snatch the bottles of champagne.

Jisung bows his head to his boss, and as he walks towards me, I turn to Todgers with my nose in the air. 'You, sir, are a colossal–' Jisung puts his arm around my shoulder, putting a stop to my tirade, and shuffles me towards the door. I ignore Todgers saying, 'Geez, what did I do?' and shrugging innocently towards his guests. We leave him to deal with the aftermath, and make a hasty exit.

Pabo

Outside, Jisung and I pause under the canopy. The rain makes a soft pattering on the canvas while I take deep breaths to calm down. Turning to me with a grin, he quips, 'Never a dull moment with you around. Let me get you away from here.'

'Thank you,' I mutter, still pumped with adrenaline. He pulls off his coat, holds it above our heads, and we run out into the evening rain.

I'm so relieved to escape that awful situation, I happily follow wherever he leads. We stop running once we get around the corner, and I try to hide that I'm out of breath already. We walk past the spa and go along a small path towards the staff accommodation village. I'm curious to see where all the staff stay, but as we approach the apartment blocks, he leads us in another direction. The path comes to an end at a wooden gate that we go through.

'Where are we going? These are getting heavy.' I hold up the champagne bottles.

'Trust me, you'll like it.'

The rain has all but stopped. He lowers his coat and puts it under his arm, takes both bottles in one hand, and his other hand takes hold of mine.

Until now, I hadn't noticed just how much I do trust him – no walls up, no guards. I feel safe and protected, looked after, and comfortable when I'm with him. I feel accepted the way I am, goofiness and all. I'm glad he's in front of me so he can't see me grinning like a Cheshire cat.

The full moon lights our way up a stony track with bushes and trees on either side. I assume we're no longer in the resort, as there is only an occasional lantern dotted along our route. It's a long uphill trek, but I resist the urge to constantly complain about my legs aching.

The dense wood gives way to a crumbling stone stairway winding up into the night. I look up to see a daunting number of steps ahead – at a steep incline. 'Please could you slow down a little bit? Your legs are much longer than mine.' I try not to whine, but I can imagine those long, muscular legs zooming effortlessly up the steps, leaving me huffing and puffing behind. He looks back over his shoulder and gives my hand a squeeze.

'Of course, sorry. Take care, the steps might be slippery.'

I'm near dead by the time we reach the top, and there's no hiding my need for oxygen. He hands me one of the bottles, and I take a few exhausted glugs. I wipe the sweat on my forehead with the back of my hand and glance around the muddy hilltop to see where we have ended up.

Unconsciously grabbing hold of Jisung's arm at the sight, I gasp. 'It's incredible.' My gaze flits between the view from this height and the man who brought me here. 'We can see the whole resort from up here, and all the pretty lights,' I gush. 'I wish Lexi was here to see. How do you know this place?'

'I come here when I need to get away. It's peaceful, beautiful.'

I marvel at the resort and beyond, sprawled below. 'Look how bright turquoise the pool is, and the hotel glowing like that, and look at all the different colours of the gardens.'

I look up to see him grinning at me as I point out the sights he's seen before.

'I told you you'd like it. Worth the trek?'

'Absolutely! It's magical! Thank you for bringing me here.' I realise I'm still holding on to Jisung's arm and reluctantly let go, turning to face him. 'And I really am very grateful to you for saving me back there. I needed to get away from that crazy woman and horrid Todgers.'

'Looked like he was the one who was about to need saving!' He laughs. 'Are you all right, though?' He leans towards me, looking concerned, and places his hand on my back. 'I'm not sure what happened, but I came as soon as I saw you had a problem.'

'I'm still shocked, but I'm all right.' A shiver runs through my body, and then I laugh. 'I can't believe I just got fired!' Oh god, I hope my editor doesn't hear about this and fire me for real. But I can't think about that when I have this perfect man all to myself, out here under the stars.

Jisung lays his coat on the ground and sits down, patting the space beside him. I hand him the unopened bottle of champagne, grab the other bottle, and sit next to him. He pops the cork and takes a swig.

'I've never drunk champagne straight from the bottle before.' He chuckles.

'Me neither.' I laugh. 'How do we say cheers in Korean?'

'Geonbae!'

'Conbeh!' I try to copy, and we chink our bottles together.

After a few drinks and a chance to give my legs a much-needed rest, I'm finally able to relax, and loudly exhale. 'You know, Todgers only brought me here because I'm not rich and I'm different from their usual clientele.'

'Hmm. I know how it feels to be different here. And no, you're not like the other guests.' Jisung lowers his head. 'You're *Pabo*... a fool. That's what makes you special.'

My head snaps towards him – was that an error in translation? I mean, I *am* a fool, but I've never been called out on it before. 'And that's a good thing?' Talk about giving me a compliment, then snatching it away again.

'Of course!' He looks up with a genuine smile. 'You don't care what anyone thinks of you... you're free.'

I stare back, trying to study his expression in the dark to see if *that* was meant as a compliment.

'You do what you want, dress how you want.' He looks down again. 'You are confident in being yourself – funny, clever, thoughtful. You have fun. I like you.'

He likes me? Did I just hear that right? A flash of heat burns from my chest to my cheeks as his words ignite a sparkler of nervous energy and thrill inside me. I look away, unable to breathe. He likes *me*? The tiny rational part of my brain realises he didn't declare his undying love, but liking me is as good as I'll ever get, and my heart explodes. I want to scream and fall backwards and kick my legs in the air. I want to star-jump and dance naked in the rain and dance naked with him... And breathe, Cally, breathe...

I slowly come back down to earth and reboot my brain. I try to consider how being free to do what I want might seem attractive to him when he's always under the spotlight. 'But I'm not on stage with everyone always watching me.' Good deflection, Cally.

'No, but as I grow older, I see what's really valuable. You're not like the women who only care about looks and fame and money. I value that in you.'

Boom! We both jump, and white sparkles erupt and fall from the sky.

'Ah, the firework display is this evening.'

'Awww, how perfect!'

More booms from below burst into brilliant glistening patterns in the darkness. We watch in a silence that I break frequently with *Ooh*s and *Aah*s. Firework enthusiasm is the ideal cover for my real, overwhelming excitement.

The display ends with an almighty finale of thunderous booms, and the sky fills with a profusion of a million colourful twinkles. It takes my breath away, and I clap with delight. When the glitter fades and the smoke clears, one last firework explodes into an enormous, magical star that shoots across the sky.

'Make a wish!' I squeal at the same time Jisung blurts out, 'Sometimes, it's me.'

'Huh?'

'Last night you asked who could think I was worthless. Well, it's me.'

With a sharp intake of breath, I whip around to face him. 'What do you mean?' I ask softly.

'Sometimes it feels like I'm finished.' He dips his gaze and twists his ring over and over. 'I was forced to leave my acting career behind in Korea a year ago. I love my job here, but sometimes I miss being back home.' He takes a sip from his bottle. I have so many questions, but first...

'I just want to say that this is just between me and you. I'm really not like that horrible reporter, I promise.'

Jisung pats my arm and nods with a 'Thanks'. I hope he knows I wouldn't betray his trust.

'How did you come to be here?'

As he twists to face me, his expression brightens. 'Ah, I met Todgers when I was working in America a few years ago. He wanted me to manage the entertainment and train the performers. I had already earned more money than I could ever need, so it worked for both of us.'

We sit in silence for a moment until a frown clouds his face. 'But I miss the challenge of acting; I don't want to play Prince Charming forever. And I miss my family.' He releases a long, heavy sigh. The sadness in his voice hurts my chest. I want to comfort him, but I know it would be inappropriate to hug him.

'What happened?' I whisper, unable to speak properly with the lump in my throat.

He stares into the distance. 'It was the media.' He nods slowly as he speaks. 'My career was taking off. I was in dramas that were very successful, and I was well known in my country. I had many interviews and TV promotions, awards, fans. I was offered excellent contracts and opportunities.' He looks around at me, and the corner of his mouth upturns. 'Acting was my dream.' But then he looks out to the darkness again and his bottom lip quivers.

He pinches between his eyes and drags his fingers down past his chin. His shoulders sink and he gets lost in his thoughts, going quiet for a while.

'It's OK if you don't want to talk.' I fight my compulsion to console him with a hand on his back, like I would with anyone else. I don't know the rules in our situation.

'No, no, I do.' His chest rises as he takes a deep breath to continue. 'At first, when I was younger, it was fun; I loved all the fans coming to see me. But I was never interested in being a celebrity. I just wanted to act. I wasn't prepared for what it meant to be an idol. Everything I did and said was watched and judged. There were more and more fans, cameras always in my face. I had to have a security team everywhere I went.' I notice his body tensing and his hands clenching.

'My schedule was secret, but sometimes there would be fans on the same plane or in the hotels. There were phone calls in the night.'

I hand him his drink. It's a small gesture, but I can see how difficult this is to remember and talk about.

'Every day there were pictures of me and with my colleagues, my friends, and every time the media said we were together, romantically. Even when I was with my sisters.' He sucks on his lower lip and frowns. 'We could never have sat out in the open like this.' He looks around at me and points behind us. 'There would be paparazzi hiding in the bushes.'

The thought makes me spin around to check. 'I can't imagine how hard that must have been for you.'

'Last night, you asked about getting married. As I got older, I wanted to settle down. My friends were getting married and having children, but I could barely date anyone. It would have to be arranged with security, all hidden. No woman wants to be kept secret.' He sighs and pauses. 'I loved my job and the money, but my life was managed by my company. I was always busy working, travelling. And they wanted me to stay single for my image.' He takes a long drink. 'The fake stories started to ruin my reputation, and the fans were angry. Whoever I was seen with was hated and attacked online.'

His shoulders hunch, and he coughs. I lean in a little closer to him, shocked by what I'm hearing and choked to hear the pain as he opens up to me. And I feel painfully ashamed of my own judgemental reaction to those photos and stories. Ashamed I was sucked in by the media's sensationalist click bait. I know better. Usually.

'My sisters were followed, and when they were put in danger...' His voice trails off to a whisper. 'It was all my fault.' He pulls his legs to him, almost humped in a ball.

'They were scared of the fans and cried when they read the lies and comments about them... My grandmother was scared to leave the house.' He wipes his cheek. I can't see if he is crying, but I have to force down the lump swelling in my throat. He straightens his body, still hugging his legs to him with his hands wringing together. 'I had to leave to keep them safe.' He wipes his cheek again and drains the remainder of his champagne.

'I was so unhappy.' His voice is low, his words seeming to tear at his throat. He stares down at his hands, gripping his ring tight. 'I promised my mother I would take care of them when she was gone,' he chokes. He turns his face to me, and now I see the wet trails down his cheeks, a deep crevice between his brows. I don't recall ever seeing a man cry before, and it hits hard. I struggle to keep my emotions under control and brush away my own tear.

'I had to get away, somewhere nobody would know me, somewhere I could live in peace. But I had to leave my family and my work behind.' The corners of his mouth tremble.

'I'm so sorry,' I whisper.

'I phone them every day. They are OK. They are safe now.' He exhales loudly, straightens his legs, and rolls back his shoulders.

I need to comfort him. I want to heal his pain. I reach over and place my hand over his, and he lets it rest there. We share a moment – of closeness, compassion, friendship. His hand turns, his fingers interlocking with mine, and we stay in that moment together, quietly, tenderly.

Without all the background noise of my everyday real life – chores, responsibilities, worries – when it's simply me and him, in this moment, everything feels right.

I squeeze his hand, and he turns to look at me. Our eyes meet, and I melt into his lingering gaze. The warmth in his face spreads to a small smile, understanding, connection.

A twinkle of light makes me tear my eyes away, then another. And then hundreds of paper lanterns begin to float up into view, illuminating the night sky like the brightest, sparkling stars. They must have been released by the resort's guests after the firework display – one must be Lexi's.

It's an unexpectedly spiritual sight, as though the lanterns are carrying away worries and releasing hopes and dreams into the universe. I rest my head against Jisung's shoulder and we watch the lanterns become tiny bright dots drifting slowly out of view.

When the sky returns to its empty darkness, Jisung flinches and lets go of my hand to check his watch.

'It's eleven o'clock.'

'Lexi. I have to get back for Nanny P by midnight.' I jump up and stretch my legs and give Jisung a hand up. When I turn to head back, Jisung grabs my wrist firmly and pulls me back to face him. My breath catches in my throat.

'Cally, wait.'

I'm not used to being manhandled, but I find it surprisingly alluring. My eyes are lost in his. Is he going to kiss me? Would I kiss him back? Of course, I have thought about kissing him, but faced with the real-life possibility, would I actually do it? I have only kissed one person for so many years, I'm not sure I even remember how. And although I no longer love Ben, I am still married.

He is still holding my wrist as he says, 'Thank you for listening. I haven't spoken to anyone about what happened, but I can be open with you.'

I'm captivated by the sincerity in his eyes.

'I feel better after talking about it all.'

My eyes flit between his intense gaze and his plump, perfectly shaped lips. He slowly pulls at my wrist, drawing me nearer. I stop breathing. His eyes close as his face gets closer to mine. I close my eyes, my heart thumping hard and fast. My tongue moistens my lips, and they purse in anticipation. I feel the warmth of his breath on my face. He presses his forehead against mine. My lips search for his.

And… he pulls away, letting go of my wrist. My eyes fly open and I jerk back. He turns and reaches for his coat. I am frozen, almost panting. He turns back towards me.

'Are you OK?'

'Hmm.' I nod. I don't know if I'm OK; I don't know anything anymore. Jisung gets his phone from his front pocket and switches on the flashlight. He takes my hand and leads our walk back.

Well, that's one question answered. Damn right I would kiss him. Right now, I would stick a cloche on my head and give myself to him on a platter. I feel awake, alive, like I'm living my best life for the first time in years. Maybe touching foreheads is a Korean thing? I push away the small twinge of confusion over whether I may have been friend-zoned – nothing is going to spoil this high. He likes me; he trusts me, and we shared intimate moments. I just need to calm my expectations. But right now, hand in hand, following Jisung down the steps, I am slamming that door of miserable marriage shut behind me and I am flying through this door that's opened. And the view is better than I could ever have thought possible.

Little Girl's Dreams

I bounce out of bed and throw open the curtains, allowing the light of a fresh new day to stream in. Lexi lifts her cute little sleepy head and mumbles, 'Five more minutes.'

I jump in the power shower, full of renewed energy and ready for new beginnings. The past few days have shown me I deserve more than a self-absorbed husband who treats me like an irrelevant housekeeper while my self-esteem drains until I feel hollow.

I visualise the rush of water washing away the layer of negativity that's accumulated from years of an unhappy marriage. I scrub away the old and welcome a new, invigorated me – free as a bird and ready to fly, ready to dream again.

This is the start of a new era of loving myself. I will accept myself as I am – scars, flaws, and all. I turn to face the bathroom mirror and squawk from the shock of my aged full-frontal nudity. Erm, yeah, I think it might take some practice to embrace those sags and wobbly bits. Baby steps, Cally, baby steps.

But one thing is for sure: if I have even the slightest chance of happiness, I have to go for it. I owe it to myself to take the risk. If I don't follow my heart, I'll spend the rest of my life wondering, *What if?* Maybe I do believe in fairy tales after all?

A firm knock at our bedroom door fills me with panic. What if it's that woman demanding payment for her dress? Or what if I'm being kicked out for the carnage in the bar last night? I'm going to get sacked, I just know it. I wait to hear if Lexi answers. A second knock suggests she's still sound asleep. I hesitantly climb out of the shower, wrap myself in a big fluffy towel, and drip my way to the door.

'Good morning, ladies.' An unexpected trolley rolls into the room, pushed by a friendly, young waiter. 'Courtesy of Fairy-Tale Wonderland.'

'Oh! How lovely!' I throw my hands up in the air, overcome by a surge of relief. 'Thank you very much!' My fears subside. For now.

'Did you sleep well, ma'am?' he asks, as though he hasn't noticed my state of undress and hair smothered in conditioner.

'Hmm, not too bad, but I dreamed I got locked in a bathroom and couldn't get home!'

'Haha, would that be so bad? You would have to live with us here.' He chuckles and nods politely as he sees himself out.

I pour a cup of coffee as a sleepy Lexi sits up and rubs her eyes.

'Aren't we spoiled, Lex?'

'This is the prettiest breakfast I've ever seen!' Lexi jumps out of bed and immediately tucks into the delectable board of strawberry-and-cream heart-shaped pastries, papaya halves filled with fruits, and bright pink smoothies. And the infamous heart-shaped pancakes covered in chocolate sauce and raspberry coulis. I'll give those ones a miss.

'Mum,' Lexi says with a mouthful of pancake, 'I don't have anything to wear to the ball.'

'Oh my gosh! We need dresses! We can hire them at the hotel gift shop. We'll go down once we're showered.' I can't resist a chocolate-covered raspberry. 'Are you excited?'

'Yes!' Lexi explodes in enthusiasm, bouncing up – ignoring the fact she almost sends breakfast flying – and babbling incoherently about her upcoming performance this evening.

We're both showered and dressed, I'm finishing a pastry, and Lexi is brushing her hair when there's another knock. 'Must be collecting the trolley.' Please don't be security. I hold my breath and open the door.

'Good morning,' sings a confident woman in pink, her blonde hair in a chic French twist. 'Your ladies-in-waiting, with the compliments of Mr Todgers.'

Mouths agape, Lexi and I stand in the middle of the bedlam as our bedroom is transformed into a busy salon. A team of porters rolls out one trolley and brings several trolleys in, plus tables, stools, and a vast assortment of equipment, with three ladies-in-waiting in total. Lexi jumps on her bed, cheering. I am speechless. Maybe this is Shitbag Todgers' way of saying sorry?

'You must be Lexi.' A fresh-faced lady in pink with brown hair scraped into a bun curtsies before the bouncing one. 'It's a pleasure to meet you, Princess Lexi. My name is Daisy. I have your ballgown here.' Lexi jumps down from her bed, sweaty and red in the face, and shocked into silence.

Daisy presents a large, flat box with a pink ribbon on top. We all gather around her and wait like excited bridesmaids while Lexi unties the ribbon, lifts the lid of the box, and holds up the cutest ruffled lilac gown with a white ribbon waistband that ties in a big bow at the back. We all gush over the pretty dress and how gorgeous Lexi will look at the ball.

And then Lexi projectile vomits.

Someone screeches that the dress is ruined. Someone else phones for an urgent clean-up team. I take Lexi's hand and shuffle her through the commotion to the bathroom and close the door.

'My poor baby, are you OK?' I help her take off her clothes and give her a wash down. 'Too much excitement?'

Lexi nods, tears in her eyes. 'Sorry.'

I give her a big hug. 'It's just a dress. I'll get you another one. Don't you worry about anything.'

Lexi squeezes me and whispers, 'Thank you, Mum.'

With a clean face and clean clothes, she's back to her usual self.

As I open the bathroom door, sounds of chaos in the bedroom stop as if someone presses an off switch. Thankfully, waiting outside is lovely, calm Daisy. After checking Lexi is all right, she places a bejewelled tiara on her head. Lexi stands tall, and her smile stretches from one ear to the other.

'Princess Lexi, if you could please come with me, it's time for rehearsals for this evening.' Daisy holds out her hand, which Lexi takes happily, and she steps away carefully as though she has books balanced on her head.

'See you later, Mum.'

'Have fun, my darling.'

The third pink lady, with long, black, wavy hair, puts her hand on my arm with a supportive smile. 'Poor little thing. Daisy will look after her.'

Both remaining women now appear to be calm with the situation under control.

'Now it's time for her mummy to be treated as a princess,' says the blonde lady in charge. I let out a little giggle.

'We have a very special day planned for you. Your first treat is a trip to the spa, if you would like to come with me?'

'Yes, please!' A huge grin is stuck to my face.

'Georgia will stay here to set up for later. My name is Abbi, by the way.'

'Hello, Abbi. I'm Cally.' I can't hold back an excited wiggle usually reserved for occasional pizza deliveries.

***

Trepidation flutters in my stomach when I face the door to the spa treatments area. I say a quick prayer to the spa gods for all to go smoothly this time, which reminds me of a certain semi-naked water god, and the smile returns to my lips.

However, all apprehension melts the moment I cross the threshold into the most tranquil of environments. Abbi leads me to a spacious treatment suite that is the epitome of pampering indulgence – a fantasia of cream flowers, creeping plants, and soft amber candlelight. An outdoor plunge pool at the far end provides a background of soothing sounds from the babbling waterfall. Now *this* is my kind of *me time*.

A glass of champagne is placed into my hand while my other hand strokes the soft, warm treatment bed strewn with pearly white petals. My shoulders relax as I inhale the sweet aromatherapeutic air and ready myself for a heavenly massage. Abbi invites me to strip down to my underwear, lie on the bed, and cover myself in a warm, fluffy towel.

I lie down, let out a long, contented breath, and close my eyes. Abbi slides the towel up to uncover my legs and I feel a hot scraping sensation down my shin – pleasant, but not as expected. I lift my head to see Abbi laying a strip of cloth over my pink leg and RIP! *Youch! Not relaxing. At. All.*

'I'll start with your lower legs and work up,' says the innocent-looking waxing torturer. Note to self: keep eyes open and watch expectations. I wonder if champagne acts as an anaesthetic and reach for my glass.

The next hour of pain and embarrassment goes past far too slowly. I discover something new to feel ashamed of – hairy toes. And I am shocked by the modern-day normals of lady gardening – I thought all that was just for porn stars. And armpit waxing is inhumane.

'You must never underestimate the power of on-point eyebrows,' Abbi tells me while the stripes of pure pain flame on my face.

Looks can be deceiving. Abbi is pretty, with lovely, big blue eyes and a cute smile. But Abbi is a monster.

Once my body has been mown, bushes hacked back, and weeds trimmed, I whimper, 'Might I be able to relax now? Please?'

'Facial and full-body massage coming right up.'

Hooray!

My face, neck, and head have never experienced such tender care. Lotions on, lotions off, potions on, potions off. Exfoliating scrubs, gentle fingertip massages, hot towels – amazing. My stomach gurgles in anticipation of my body receiving similar attention.

Upon the first strokes of Abbi's oily hands on my back, she is forgiven. Her magical touch kneads away the tension and stress, and I finally achieve the elusive state of relaxation.

I appreciate this calm before the brewing storm. It's a lot easier to move on from a breakup when the other person doesn't even know yet. If only I could fast forward the next few days, weeks, months of hard stuff. I can only hope he'll leave quietly. Maybe he'll relish cutting the ties that hold him back. Not that his wedding ring has held him back – it's been in a drawer for years.

Increased stomach burbling draws my attention, and I become concerned that it may not be excitement – it might be trapped gas. And while the pressure of the massage is muscle ecstasy, each sweep of my lower back increases the urge to expel said gas. Just my luck. Thanks, fart gods. But despite my buttocks' preventative tension, I surrender to the spa's relaxed ambience and close my eyes.

I awake with a start when Abbi asks me to turn over. I flip onto my back and am relieved I no longer need to pass wind. Oh no. Although Abbi doesn't say anything, I hate to imagine what happened while I was asleep. As my daughter would say: *Cringe!*

***

Back in our bedroom salon, refreshed and renewed, I find lunch waiting. A spectacularly presented silver tray decorated with a rainbow of crystals and gemstones sur-rounds... a bowl of steaming water with flowers floating on top and a clear crystal at the bottom. Georgia notices my dubious expression.

'It's full of nutrients, antioxidants, and positive en-ergy. Just don't eat the quartz in the bowl,' she says with a reassuring smile. Water and flowers for lunch it is then. I chew on a tasteless white flower and take a sip of hot water. What the...? What is this mystical brew? How is it possible for clear water to have such a delicious fla-vour of tomato and basil? Magic is the only plausible ex-planation.

It's only after I am replenished with the magical elixir of life that I notice the large, flat, black box tied with red ribbon lying on my bed. I dart over to read the gift tag.

For the woman with fire in her eyes,
with my sincere apologies
Frank

I flick away the tag. Well, at least he's acknowledged he was out of order. Georgia tucks her hair behind her ear, looking uncomfortable. 'The big boss.' Her voice lowers to a whisper. 'Yeah, he has a habit of rubbing people up the wrong way.' She's interrupted by Abbi rushing into the room and screeching, 'Wait!'

My head whips around to see her throwing her hands up in panic, knocking strands of hair out from her perfectly neat up-do.

'It's not time to reveal the dress yet!'

I jump back, laughing at Abbi's over-reaction.

'We have to stick to the schedule!' Abbi moves the box before I can peep inside. 'Mr Todgers personally chose the dress. We can't ruin the surprise.'

I look to Georgia with fear in my eyes. 'Mr Todgers chose my dress?' I mouth silently.

'You'll love it,' she reassures. 'It's worth a fortune!'

I sit on the bed, head spinning. What the hell did he choose for me? A maid's uniform? It feels as odd and scary as someone else choosing a bride's wedding dress. He doesn't know about my lifelong obsession with the blue Cinderella dress that I would have picked. And anyway, that would mean him dressing me like his niece, which is weird and wrong on so many levels.

Fire in my eyes. What does he mean? Anger? Passion? Or just red and bloodshot?

Still, I'm glad he's apologised. It doesn't make it acceptable for him to fire me instead of standing up for me, but the very last thing I want to do is make a fuss and kiss my promotion goodbye. I'm proud I stood up for myself, but I'd rather forget the whole embarrassing incident ever happened. So I'll quietly and gratefully accept our holiday of a lifetime and all these gifts, and now my dress for the ball.

Todgers was never quite what I imagined when I wished for a fairy godmother.

***

Lexi returns from rehearsals in high spirits, and our lovely ladies-in-waiting spring into action.

'Who's ready for a princess pampering?' Abbi hands us soft white dressing gowns to change into and seats us next to each other in our pop-up salon. Lexi is effervescent. I'm not quite sure how she will sit still long enough to be pampered.

But as it turns out, Daisy is a skilled super-nanny beautician, able to keep Lexi entertained and occupied while she paints nails. Poor Daisy. Her brain will be frazzled in no time as soon as my darling daughter starts talking *non-stop*. I sit back, giggling to myself, while the nails on my hairless toes are painted a beautiful shade of deep red.

While my toenails are drying, Lexi turns to face me, waving her wet fingernails through the air.

'Mum, I need some kind of relationship advice.'

My heart bursts. She looks and sounds so grown up. 'Of course, darling.' Although this week I have demonstrated I am the last person who should be giving relationship advice, I am keen to hear about her very first crush now she has discovered boys.

'Is it about Jack?'

'Who?'

'Jack and the beanstalk, Jack.'

'No! I don't like him anymore. This is about Baby Bear.'

'Ah, from the three bears, OK.' I am secretly pleased. Having a crush on a bear is far more preferable than on a boy. I want her to hold on to her precious innocence a little longer. I can't deal with my *own* angst, let alone all the teenage boyfriend troubles she will no doubt have to face.

'All the girls are having a competition to see who will get to dance with Baby Bear at the ball, and I really want it to be me but I don't know if he will ask me.'

'Well then, you ask him! You don't need to wait around for a boy – I mean, bear – to call the shots.'

Lexi smiles with a new look of determination in her eyes. 'Thanks, Mum, I will.'

I feel both stunned and smug. I did a good mum thing! I said something that wasn't embarrassing or uncool (or whatever word I'm supposed to use these days).

My smile fades at the odd look on Lexi's face. She stares at me for a few moments, then leans closer and sheepishly says, 'Mum, can I tell you a secret?'

'Of course you can, Lex. You can tell me anything. What's bothering you?'

'I don't want to ruin it for you, but I know something about Baby Bear.'

Intrigue, worry, and a whole bunch of thoughts run through my head that I'd rather not think about. 'What is it?'

'Baby Bear isn't really a boy.'

I think I am supposed to look shocked as she continues to whisper.

'He's actually a lady in a suit. I saw her take off her bear head. I still want to dance with them though. But promise you won't tell anyone.'

I pretend to zip my mouth while trying not to laugh. It's cute she didn't want to spoil the magic for me.

Then I'm struck with an idea of how to be a super mum. 'Lex, I just need to pop downstairs quickly.'

Abbi is standing in the doorway holding her tight schedule. I whisper to her as I pass, then run down the stairs, still wearing my dressing gown and without shoes, so I don't smudge the varnish. I am on a covert super-mum mission. I weave through the team of decorators preparing the grand staircase for tonight's big event, pulse quickening at the secret delights in store for my darling daughter.

***

The shop is quietly tucked around the side of the hotel with a modest window display of children's fairy-tale books and toys. I step inside the door, and I'm pretty sure my eyes become heart-shaped. I am in a peacock-coloured Aladdin's cave of sparkling delights that surpasses my inner six-year-old's wildest dreams. I am in fairy princess shopping heaven – a shop full of things that either didn't exist back in the dark ages when I was a child, or were things that only other children had. And now, I want to touch and try and buy *everything!*

My eyes flit from the rainbow of puffy ball gowns next to an enormous golden mirror to the glistening tiaras and the wall of glimmering diamond necklaces.

'May I help you, Cally?'

'Thalia! What a lovely surprise!'

She doesn't mention my outfit, or lack of. Either the staff here are all extremely polite or they are used to seeing guests in different states of undress.

'I would love some help; I have lots of gifts to buy,' I sing, exhilarated to begin the shopping trip of a lifetime. All courtesy of Ben. I'm so glad I brought his personal savings account card in case of emergencies. And this is most definitely a fairy-tale emergency.

First, I'll treat Lexi to a new ballgown that will make my little girl's wishes come true. I know the exact type of dress – we've imagined it together during so many bedtime chats. Thalia helps me find the one – elegant, sophisticated, and fit for a young lady, without a hint of a frill or bow or anything that might suggest she is a – gasp – child.

My heart swells with warmth at the perfect pale-blue evening gown – with little blue sparkly flowers around the neckline and capped sleeves, a tulle overlay with larger blue flowers around the hem, and with a puffy, but not too puffy, floor-length skirt. I feel all warm and fuzzy inside, and even fuzzier when I see a matching lightweight tiara that she will be able to comfortably dance in. Thank you, Ben. It's about time you made our wonderful daughter feel special.

Now it's time to make another little girl's dreams come true. The young me who desperately yearned for the blue dress. But I'm a big girl now, which can mean only one thing… shoes!

I immediately spot them – the sparkliest, most impractical high heels, which deserve to be displayed in a glass case and worshipped for the rest of my days. And clear crystals should hopefully go with any dress that Todgers has picked. There are no price labels. I guess at an exclusive resort, if you have to ask… These beauties must cost more than all my worldly possessions combined, which makes them all the more irresistible.

I almost skip to the pink-upholstered, golden throne to try them on. I first check the polish on my toes has dried, then carefully put each foot inside. When they fit and I view them in the mirror, they bring a tear to my eye. I feel light-headed placing them on the counter for wrapping. This must be what elation feels like. I'm in shoe heaven!

Thalia draws my attention to a matching crystal clutch bag, and I place it on the counter. This is compensation for all the times Ben ignored me and Lexi and took us for granted. Then I select the most gorgeous, eye-catching necklace. This is for his cruel words and all the times he put me down. Finally, I pick some matching sparkly earrings. These are for all the times he saw me cry and turned his back.

Fantasy shopping is incredibly cathartic.

Next, a gift for Nanny P. She's been a blessing this week, and I can't wait to give her a little thank-you present.

'Thalia, what would you choose as the best gift?'

'Ooh! I know! I know!' she coos. 'I've always loved this gorgeous bracelet.'

Her face lights up as she points to a dainty gold chain dotted with emerald flowers with small diamond centres. Perfect. I select the blue sapphire one to match Nanny P's eyes and ask for the emerald bracelet to be wrapped as well.

The jewellery pieces are placed in peacock-blue velvet boxes and tied with pink ribbons. Without so much as a glance at the total cost, I tap in Ben's pin, which he helpfully had on a post-it note stuck to the back.

Thalia arranges a porter to deliver the hauls of my shopping spree to our room. Then I take her by the hand.

'Thank you for your kindness and support this week, Thalia. You are a treasure, and I would like to give you a gift to show my appreciation.' I hand her the little box containing the emerald bracelet. She flies around the counter and throws her arms around me, blubbing a thank you into my shoulder.

'Don't cry!' I pat her on the back and sniff. 'You'll start me off!'

She steps back and wipes the happy tears from her eyes.

'Ooh! One last thing. Please could you teach me how to curtsy?'

One curtsy lesson and a hug later and I leave the magic shop, stopping at reception to have a quick word with Diane.

SATURDAY

Fire in Her Eyes

'Oh Lexi, look at you!' I rush to take a closer look. Her long, boisterous curls have been tamed and styled into glossy ringlets. 'You look amazing!' I hug her shoulders, not wanting to put a single ringlet out of place. She has a hint of sparkle around her big blue eyes and a touch of pink on her lips. She is almost ready to join the other children for dinner and dancing.

Abbi answers a knock at the door.

'Special delivery for Princess Lexi.' The porter hands the silver garment bag to Abbi. I scamper to the door to collect the boxes while the leading lady-in-waiting looks a little fraught at the changes to her meticulous plans.

We gather around as Lexi steps forward to receive her gift. I hold my breath waiting for her reaction as Abbi unzips the bag.

Lexi's eyes widen with wonder as the gown is uncovered, and she lets out an elated gasp. 'Oh Mum, it's perfect!' She flings her arms around me, delighted tears slipping down her plump cheeks. I squeeze her in a tight hug, my heart swelling with joy at her reaction.

We help Lexi into the dress, each layer eliciting fresh explosions of giggles as the fairy-tale ballgown comes together. With the tiara secured in her glossy curls, Lexi gives us a twirl. Her eyes sparkle with delight as the ballgown billows around her. The sound of her laughter is so joyful and contagious, we are all caught up in her magical moment. 'Oh my darling, you look beautiful,' I whisper, hand on heart. Childhood really does pass by in the blink of an eye. My baby girl is now a stunning young woman.

The ladies-in-waiting flood her with compliments, even Abbi, despite her plans going awry. There's another knock at the door, which Abbi goes to answer.

With great timing, Baby Bear pads into the room, escorted by Mummy Bear, Daddy Bear, and a photographer snapping away. Lexi pales, and I fear she may vomit again. I stand beside her and squeeze her hand. Baby Bear kneels before Lexi and takes her other hand in his paw.

'Princess Lexi, please would you do me the honour of accompanying me to the ball?' His voice is gentle and sweet, and I'm thrilled this wonderful experience is being captured on camera. Lexi has a moment of shyness and nods in response to the invitation. She faces me with a look of disbelief that flourishes into an exhilarated glow. My heart explodes.

'Daddy Bear and I will take these youngsters down to dinner,' says Mummy Bear.

'You have a special treat lined up after your performance, Princess Lexi,' Daddy Bear says gruffly. 'There will be a horse and carriage waiting to take you and Baby Bear on an adventure around the grounds before the ball begins.'

Baby Bear throws his paws in the air. 'Wow! This evening's going to be just right,' he says in his cute little voice.

Lexi is still quietly stunned, but thankfully all remains quiet on the vomiting front. We have goodbye kisses, and as we wave them off, she warms up and I hear her and Baby Bear chatting away down the corridor. I expect this will be the best night of her life so far.

Abbi puts her hand on my shoulder and whispers, 'Was that your doing?'

'It was.' I beam. 'I'm sorry about the other dress.'

'You did an awesome job. And now it's your turn to transform into a princess.'

'Can I see my dress now?'

'Glow-up first.' Abbi is such a tease.

It may be a little excessive to have three ladies-in-waiting all to myself, but I need all the help I can get to look fit for a ball.

'Champagne. Relax, we've got this.' Daisy hands me a glass. This week seems to have revolved around champagne, but right now I welcome its help to calm the butterflies in my stomach. Tonight is *the* night. The ball of my childhood dreams. And today, the new, free, courageous me will be spreading my wings at the ball of my adult fantasies.

Georgia is painting my fingernails, Abbi is curling my hair ready to create a relaxed half up-do with curls individually coiled and held with sparkling pins. Daisy is waiting to paint my face.

'Ladies, will you join me for a glass of champagne? I don't like to drink alone, and you deserve a treat for all your hard work today.'

Abbi declines, but three pairs of big doe eyes and three pouts later, she's won around.

'To Princess Cally. May you have the best night ever,' Daisy toasts.

'Cheers, ladies.'

The atmosphere in the room relaxes, and I love having friendly adults around for some fun, idle chatter. I'm curious: 'Have you ever been to the ball yourselves?'

Georgia laughs. 'God, no! It's not for the likes of us.'

Hearing her words, doubts and fears crowd in. The ball's not for the likes of me either, work or no work. It's still going to be the same me regardless of any dress and however much make-up they slap on my face. The thought of sitting through a formal dinner, single, and without the focus of our children's company, fills me with dread. My nerves are frayed enough. I don't think I could cope with the additional social anxiety of making small talk with strangers.

'I'm skipping dinner.'

Shocked gasps erupt around me, but the tension in my shoulders immediately melts away. 'Who fancies room service? My treat.'

After a moment's silence, there are two squeals and a small, pleading, 'Boss?' from Daisy. Abbi sighs and pretends to screw up her schedule and throw it over her shoulder. 'Go on then.'

'Yay, Abbi! Georgia, do you want to grab the menu? Pick whatever you like – it's all on expenses!' Laughter rings out and I breathe out a big, satisfied sigh, feeling a hundred times lighter after making this decision. A girlie party with *my people,* and without a single diamond between us, is just what I need.

While we wait for our party food to arrive, Daisy starts work on my face. All the mirrors are covered for the big surprise reveal once I'm ready. I had no idea one face could need so many products: mists, primers, powders, undercoats, overcoats, and a ridiculous number of brushes.

'You have gorgeous eyes. You're so lucky, having such lovely long lashes,' Daisy says, tickling my eyelid with one of the brushes.

'Are you sure I won't look like a pantomime dame?' I ask in all seriousness, but Daisy looks aghast at the mere suggestion.

I laugh. 'You haven't seen my make-up skills – it wouldn't be the first time.'

'Oh, you silly!' She taps the end of my nose with a giggle, showing her cute dimples. 'You're going to knock 'em dead!'

Mid-make-up session, our trolley load of food arrives – pizza for me, a hunk of steak with chips for Georgia, three exotic desserts for Daisy, a plate of oysters for Abbi, plus a bottle of champagne. We clear one of the beautician's tables to create a makeshift dining area, and I hand around our traffic-light-coloured cocktails. 'Cheers, ladies. Thank you for everything.'

Georgia raises her glass. 'Cheers to you, Cally.'

Daisy nudges up to my arm as she raises her glass. 'Don't get me wrong, I adore my job, but it's the guests who treat us like real people and not servants, they're the ones who make it really special. So, thank you.'

Awww. Daisy's so sweet, it's hard not to pinch her cute, dimpled cheeks.

'Cheers!' The four of us chink our glasses, eyeing Daisy's indulgent food selection.

'I couldn't decide!' She giggles.

We watch Abbi slurp her hideous-looking choice. 'What? I've always wanted to try oysters.'

Georgia frowns and puts down her knife and fork. 'Do you think we'll get into trouble?'

'Who's going to know?' I say, reeling in a never-ending string of mozzarella from my slice of pizza while trying not to ruin my make-up. 'And if anyone says anything' – I put on my poshest voice – 'you can tell them I demanded you party with me!'

'All the staff are good at keeping secrets anyway,' Daisy says, licking cream from her lips.

'Daisy!' Abbi looks sternly at her, a warning tone in her voice, before saying sweetly, 'Cally's a journalist, remember?'

'Aww, Abbi. I'm not going to say anything!' I assure her. Daisy's eyes flit between the two of us until Abbi blinks her heavily mascaraed eyelashes long and hard, giving the go-ahead for Daisy to spill the beans.

'Is this the gossip being kept on the *DL*?' I whisper, super excited that I might find out at last. Daisy nods.

'The staff village is a party village at night. Most of the guests are either in their rooms or the bar, so no one ever knows!'

'Ha ha!' My eyes light up. I knew all these youngsters couldn't be as perfect as they seem! 'Go on...!'

Daisy leans close, eyes shining with mischief. 'We keep all the full wine bottles the guests leave at meal-times, and the guys snaffle a few crates from stores.'

Georgia chimes in with a giggle and raises her glass. 'Party time in the dorms!'

'And...' Daisy pauses while she finishes her cocktail, drawing me in closer for what seems like the big reveal. 'Staff relationships are against the rules, so instead, the girls have a points system.'

I tilt my head and quickly swallow my mouthful. 'Points for what?'

'Well... we get points for pulling the guys.' Georgia joins in with the goss, flicking her shiny hair back over her shoulder. 'Like we get one point for snogging one of the team, three points for kissing one of the main cast, and five points for a guest.'

'Shakira!' I screech, causing three looks of con-fusion. 'Oh, sorry, stupid habit. I've been trying not to swear.' With wide eyes, I flap my pizza. 'Tell me more!'

The atmosphere becomes full-on boozy hen-night hilarity. 'Do many people score the five points?'

'Oh, yeah!' All three ladies laugh. I'm shocked, hor-rified, kind of impressed, and highly amused.

'You should see Abbi out on the prowl when the new guests arrive!' Daisy giggles.

Abbi turns away nonchalantly, then looks back at us with the cheekiest grin and slowly puckers her lips. 'And I am proud to say I'm top of the scoreboard.'

'Abbi!' I scream. 'You dark horse! You think you know someone after they've been up close and personal with your bikini line, but obviously not!'

We fall about laughing and raise a toast to the current winner. I am nervous to ask but have to find out. 'And the main cast?'

'Nah, they're no fun. They never want to play.' Daisy has no idea what a relief that is to hear. If they only knew what I've been up to. Abbi has lust in her eyes as she sighs and shakes her head. 'But what I wouldn't do to get my hands on that Prince Charming!'

The conversation is nearing dangerous territory, but how I would love to be able to talk to someone about my crazy week. This impromptu party makes me realise how much I miss having a group of work colleagues.

'I envy you lovely girls. It must be such a laugh living in this amazing place, working together and having fun.' I take the champagne bottle from the ice bucket and unwrap the top. 'Oh, to be young again!'

'You're still young!' Abbi scoffs, taking the bottle from my hands, expertly popping the cork, and pouring our drinks.

Georgia holds her fork suspended mid-air, her mouth open wide, still full of chips. 'But you've got it all! Married, kids, well, kid, and an amazing job that pays you to come here as a VIP.'

She pauses to chew and swallow, and Abbi takes over. 'I can't wait to be settled down, like you.'

I pretend to joke. 'It's not all it's cracked up to be.'

'I want to have four kids.' Daisy begins a conversation with the others about the children's names she's already chosen.

I'm stumped. If I already have it all, why isn't it enough? Why do I need so much more?

Abbi finishes her drink, shakes out her long hair, and re-pins the style in a matter of seconds – it would take me a good hour if I tried, and my hair would still look like a bird's nest. She glances at her watch and screams, 'Oh my god! The time!' She jumps up, instantly switching back to professional mode. 'We need to get you downstairs right now!'

I'm standing in the middle of the immediate flurry of action, holding a pizza crust to my mouth. The ladies flap around, clearing our party away, poking at my hair, removing my robe, and shrieking about preparing me to go to watch the children.

When I twig what's happening, I throw my crust in a panic. 'I can't miss Lexi's show!' Hearing her performance is only moments away sends my heart racing. 'But I'm not even dressed!' I have to shout to be heard.

'We're not ready for your dress.' Abbi's voice rises to a fever pitch.

'Wait. The kit from the photoshoot is here somewhere.' Daisy scours her boxes of equipment and pulls out a robe. Within seconds, I'm steered out of the room and stuffed into the lift with Abbi.

I finally get to take a breath, but then catch sight of my reflection on the glass door. I elicit a gasp-scream-snort sound that I hope I never have to make again. Followed by hysterical laughter. One eye fully made up, and hair half pinned on the opposite side. But the robe is something else.

I look down at the hot-pink satin negligee-style robe, tears rolling down my face as I tie the belt. I swoop my frilly-cuffed, wizard-sleeved arm and purr, 'Daaaaaarling!' at Abbi, who can't hold in her laughter any longer.

I flounce in my long, flowing, ruffled robe, looking like a romance novelist who spends her days lounging on a chaise longue, drinking martinis, and tapping on an old-fashioned typewriter.

'Can I keep it, Abbi?' I gasp through my guffaws. 'Forget working at home in my pyjamas. I think I've found my new style.' We giggle as we walk past staring guests, all the way through the hotel. Until we get to the ballroom.

If Lexi sees how I look in public, or more importantly, if her friends see me, it will be game over. Abbi leaves me at the door, and I sneak inside to hide at the back of the crowd of parents.

Acting out short fairy-tale sketches with songs and dances, the children are adorable. Lexi is in her element, and her beaming smile shows she's enjoying every second. With tears in my eyes, my heart swells with pride at how far she's come this week. Arriving as a child full of sadness, she performs here as a young lady brimming with confidence.

As the performance draws to an end, excitement ripples through the group of kids as they're joined by the entertainment cast. I duck down out of view of Prince Charming while also trying to catch glimpses of him through tiny gaps between parents.

There's no doubt that I look odd and unfortunately attract the attention of the dad next to me. Of course, that would be the point my satin belt slips undone, giving him an eyeful that makes him blush. However, playing peek-a-boob with a stranger barely makes the top ten of this week's embarrassing moments.

I'm far more concerned with getting the timing just right to see the end of the show and then make a discreet dash before Lexi sees how I'm dressed. I glance around at the distracting mumbling by my side to find the evil eye directed straight at me. From the few words I can make out, blushing dad's wife caught him staring at me. Her elbow sharply digs into his side and her icy scowl makes Lexi's glares seem lacklustre in comparison. I think it might be best if I move.

I shuffle along to a safer hideout amongst the crowd and stand up straight before my back seizes. There I meet the sparkling eyes of my dreamy prince, which send heat all through my body. He's so utterly perfect. My chest rises in a huge, swoony sigh, making my belt slip undone again. Thankfully, I don't see any dads blushing while I tie it back up in a triple knot. Not that I would notice with my eyes fixed on his smile as he looks down, all shy and cute.

I also hadn't noticed the children making their way towards their parents until Lexi is almost upon me. It's too late to run or hide. I pull her into my arms before she can pretend not to know me. 'Well done, my darling. That was a wonderful performance. I'm so proud of you.'

'Thanks, Mum.' Lexi's voice is muffled against me. 'Err... I can't breathe.'

Forced to release her, I let Lexi step back. Her eyes widen and she gulps. 'Is... Is that your ballgown?' She asks most politely, stroking the smooth, shiny material. 'Or are you a princess wizard?'

'It's just a robe. I was in the middle of getting ready and I didn't want to miss any of your show.' I can't resist boinging her beautiful ringlets. 'I'm so sorry. I hope you don't mind too much?' My eyes squint in preparation for a *You've ruined my life* outburst.

Instead, Lexi throws her arms around my neck and gives me a huge hug. 'Thank you for coming to watch me, Mum.' She reaches up and gives me a kiss on the cheek. I wrap my arms around her and squeeze her tightly, my mummy heart overwhelmed with emotion. I breathe in her familiar scent as her soft hair brushes against my cheek. Letting out a constrained sob, I close my eyes and savour this most precious moment.

As she pulls away from my grip, her beautiful smiling face contorts to a look of confusion. I try to laugh, my nose congested from holding in my sentimental blubbering. 'Someone must be chopping onions.'

Still frowning, she looks around for a strange onion-chopper, making me giggle. Then excitedly exclaims, 'Baby Bear!'

A path clears through the crowd, making way for Baby Bear to approach Lexi and deliver a ceremonious bow with a flourish and grand sweep of his arm.

'Princess Lexi, it's adventure time!'

She squeals and curtsies. Then, on hearing the cheers and clapping from the other children, turns and curtsies to them too.

'Our carriage awaits. Are you ready to go?'

She yells a loud 'Yes!' and links her arm in his. Before they skip out of the door, she calls back, 'Tell you all about it later, Mum. I can't wait to see your dress. Byeee!'

***

Welcoming me back into the bedroom, Abbi claps her hands.

'Right! We've got a princess to make.'

Once my hair and make-up are complete and sym-metrical, I jump up, tingling in anticipation. 'Dress?'

'Dress.' Abbi nods and fetches the box. She reads out loud: 'For the woman with fire in her eyes.'

A hush falls as Abbi lays the box down. Hands trembling, I untie the bow and lift the lid.

Red sparkles steal my breath. Raising the dress, Abbi lifts it high to see its full glory. Gasps fill the room, and my hand flies to my heart as I stumble backwards. The dress is made of all my dreams and wishes, and fairy-tale magic.

'Thank you, Mr Shitbag,' I whisper. He has surpris-ingly amazing taste – a deep-red, floor-length ball gown, strapless with a pointed sweetheart neckline and a corset back. The bodice sparkles with sequins and the full skirt has a subtle glittery overlay. Stunning.

I desperately hope it fits. 'Fat pants!' I yell, and scramble towards my suitcase. The ladies look at me, confused. 'I need my shape wear! Got to hold in all these jiggly bits somehow.'

Georgia scoffs. 'You've got a great hourglass fig-ure. I'd love to have some curves. I'm just straight up and down.'

She helps me haul my case onto the bed and as I open it, a stack of freebie toiletries tumbles out. I hear giggles as I quickly shove the lovely complimentary soaps and lotions back in, my cheeks burning. Lexi must have been storing them each day before they're replaced by the housekeepers. Oh well, I'm sure these ladies would do the same. I rummage around for the new lacy fat pants I brought for emergencies.

Ten seconds later, I emerge from the bathroom, laughing. 'They only fit one leg!' I'll have to make do with my old big black bloomer fat pants to prevent any bottom jiggling.

Daisy fixes the last of my make-up with a slick of deep red gloss, Abbi completes the finishing touches to my hair, and Georgia helps me with the new jewellery. With a squeal, I step into my fabulous sparkling shoes – the shoes of the new, strong, confident Cally.

They all help me into the underskirts and, finally, my gown. Thankfully, the bodice has plenty of inner scaffolding in the absence of a bra.

'Ready?' Abbi pulls the corset ribbons with all her might. The dress fits – who needs to breathe, anyway? My boobs are squished up to my neck, so the ladies make adjustments to make the bodice look less pornographic. With a spray of perfume, I am ready and feeling good. Now to see what I look like...

Abbi steps out to collect a full-length mirror from the corridor. I close my eyes, feeling incredibly nervous, visions of dames and drag queens swirling in my mind.

'Princess Cally, open your eyes!'

I force one eye open and see a blur of red. I force my second eye open and my jaw drops. I stare at the princess in the reflection, and tears collect in my eyes.

'No crying! You'll smudge your make-up!' Daisy says, with tears in her own eyes.

I hold my head up and take a deep breath, or as deep as my corset allows. 'What a transformation!'

My dress is perfect. I swish the skirts to get another peek at my new shoes, then look up to my hair. Wow! It looks incredible. My eye make-up is subtle, my lips bold and beautiful. I step closer to the mirror and stare at my reflection. 'Wait!' I whirl back around to Daisy. 'Where did my wrinkles go? I look ten years younger.' I stare back at my reflection in disbelief.

Daisy giggles. 'That's our special facial and miracle serum.'

'What is this magic serum? Can I buy it? I'll take all the stock you have.' I turn my head, looking at myself from all angles. OK, I'm going to say it...

'I look amazing!'

My yell is met with a trio of jubilant cheers and whoops. 'You did it, ladies. Thank you so much!' I pull them all into a celebratory group hug.

'OK then, time to go to the ball! I'll help you with your dress going down the stairs,' Abbi offers.

'And Daisy and I will pack up – you'll never know we were here,' says Georgia.

'Thank you all.' I unbox my sparkly bag, pop in the lip gloss, and off I totter.

'Have fun!'

'Don't do anything we wouldn't do!'

***

Abbi and I stand at the top of the staircase, and I take a few deep breaths.

'It feels like I'm about to get married!'

'And I'm giving you away!' Abbi laughs.

I have a sudden flashback to my wedding day all those years ago – the closed doors of the registry office, me in my no-frills, secondhand dress. Young and naïve, with big dreams and high hopes. The doors opening and Mother pulling me through so I didn't bolt from nerves. But now, although filled with butterflies, I want to be seen. And I even want my photo taken to capture this occasion when I look and feel better than I could ever imagine.

Abbi lifts my skirts, and I concentrate on keeping my balance. We make our way down the incredible staircase that is decorated with cascading white roses and candles. Cameras are clicking. I raise my head and smile, clinging to the bannister so I don't tumble. 'I can do this,' I repeat to myself over and over.

When we reach the lobby, Abbi gives me a hug. 'You've got this. Have a fantastic night.'

I'm alone on the red carpet, which I follow outside and through a beautiful tunnel of white drapes, hanging wisteria, and chandeliers. I pass a huge marquee where the catering ninjas are clearing up after dinner, and then I stand before the closed doors of the ballroom.

Todgers may have been onto something when he said I had fire in my eyes. I no longer feel burnt out. Fiery passion inside burns brighter than my fears, and I'm ready to play with fire. I'm...

... taking off my wedding ring. I twist it off my finger, rub at the indents it leaves, and slip it in my bag. Maybe I should feel sad or feel *something*, at least, and while the prospect of starting over is daunting, the thought of staying trapped is terrifying. But today, I'm a phoenix rising from the ashes. With power brows.

The Ball

T he ballroom doors swing open. Todgers, with a footman either side, forms the welcoming party. He stares, shaking his head, and mutters, 'Incredible.' He takes my hand and greets me with air kisses, then steps back to ogle me as if admiring his handiwork.

'Don't you scrub up well? Just incredible.'

'Frank.' I give a curt nod. His reaction makes me feel powerful enough to be on first-name terms. He's not quite drooling, but I imagine in a different environment, he might be on his knees, begging to lick my boots about now. Revolting man. I clear my throat, and he gathers his composure.

'Ms Cathy Jackson,' he announces. My eyes roll and I prise my hand from his grip to take a glass of champagne from the approaching waiter.

Gliding the red carpet, I pause before the wall of white roses, unleashing my best celebrity smile for the photographer. I find the nearest bar table, set down my glass, and scan the colourful ballgowns and tuxedos, the band, exquisite decor. My breath is fast and shallow, my chest buzzing. My first ball. *The* ball. The beginning of my new life. I look the part and feel confident – the polar opposite of when I came to the welcome meeting, which seems a lifetime ago. And maybe this time, Prince Charming will be looking out to see *me*.

I follow the tables around the edge of the ballroom looking for Lexi and Baby Bear. I still need to confirm his intentions are honourable, I giggle to myself. The enormous room looks extraordinary, swathed in a dim pink glow. Dark-pink flowers and twinkling lights drip from the ceiling and weave their way down trees on each corner of a central square, culminating in a transparent dance floor with a sea of flowers beneath.

I spot the group of yummy mummies wearing sleek, body-sculpting gowns in complementary muted tones. Against the background of floral table displays and candlelight, they could easily pass as models on a photoshoot. Maybe they are? Maybe the robe was for one of them? Miss Sugar Daddy catches my gaze and points me out to the others. They all look over and smile – genuine smiles that lift my spirits further, and I beam back.

On the other side of the dance floor, I spot Lexi, and am about to cross over when the crowd parts. Prince Charming steps forward. Our eyes meet across the sea of dancers and time stands still. He doesn't even try to hide his gasp as he looks me up and down. My heart races, and I lower my head in an attempt to hide my cheeks flushing the colour of my dress.

My dashing Prince Charming, dressed in a majestic outfit of a white ruffled shirt beneath a long, intricately embroidered, silver waistcoat, a knee-length, collarless, metallic-grey coat, and tall boots. He bows before me and I curtsy, correctly.

Without a word, he presents a beautiful red rose from behind his back, which he slides into my hair. Then, with a gorgeous smile and a twinkle in his eyes, he takes my hand and leads me to the dance floor.

I can barely breathe. This is *the* moment. The realisation of my childhood dreams. At long last, it's my turn to be the princess who gets her prince.

The cocktail of nerves and excitement is almost too much to bear, and as he pulls me close, I am sure he can feel my heart beating through my corset. He leans his head towards mine and his lips brush my ear as he whispers, 'You look ravishing... My Belle of the Ball.'

The room spins as he twirls me around, catching me in his arms as I dizzily whirl in my heels. I can't help but stare into his beautiful eyes for longer than socially acceptable. When I dreamed of this moment last night, this was when he kissed me. He beams and leans his head in close. 'Just let me lead. You'll be great.'

Somehow my feet remember to move as we practised, and we glide across the floor in perfect unison, as if our feet never touch the ground. The rest of the room fades away to just the two of us, bodies pressed together, connected. Our eyes are locked, my fingers tingle in his grasp, and his firm grip around my waist makes me feel like I'm floating on air. He smells delicious, and I breathe him in. This moment is everything I've ever dreamed of and I never want it to end. My Prince Charming. My heart is his.

As we twirl, my eyes briefly flit towards movement over his shoulder, breaking the trance. The yummy mummies are cheering me on with thumbs up and clapping. I guess they're impressed I've bagged the most desirable dance partner.

With just that split second's lapse in concentration, I step out of time and can't catch up with the dance steps. Jisung and I laugh and stop at a nearby table.

I tear my eyes from his to look around for Lexi and spot her running towards the marquee with a group of girls. The children look to be having the best night, laughing and playing games.

Prince Charming takes two glasses from a passing tray, and our fingers gently touch as he places a drink in my hand.

I take a sip of bubbly courage to still the swirl of nervous knots in my stomach.

It is now or never.

'Can I speak to you in confidence?' I ask with mock self-assurance.

'Sure!' He looks at me curiously.

Stifling an embarrassed giggle behind manicured fingers, I lower my head, my heart pounding as I gather every ounce of courage I possess.

He laughs. 'What is it?'

'Ahem.' I regain my composure. I glance up at his friendly face and take a deep breath.

'I have a huge crush on you.' I bite my lip, shocked at my own boldness as he gives a bashful grin. 'And as it's my last night here, I want to ask you a question I've never asked anyone before.' I check no one nearby can hear.

'Oh?' He raises an eyebrow, looking bemused.

I've come this far. At this point, I have nothing to lose.

'Haha.' I titter, inwardly smacking my head, trying to knock some sense into my middle-aged brain. And yet I continue.

'I wanted to suggest a secret, illicit rendezvous.'

The words are out. There's no turning back.

I wait breathlessly for his response and smirk like it is no big deal, funny, even. As cool and calm as ever, his lips curl to match my cheery expression, although his eyes look at me seriously as he hesitates.

'Yeah... No,' he says slowly, as it dawns on him what I am suggesting.

No.

The word hangs in the air between us.

'No,' I agree, continuing to feign amusement and trying to maintain eye contact. But my cheeks twitch as the smile drains from my face.

No.

The word strikes me with a force that steals the breath from my lungs and echoes through my head. It rips out my heart and extinguishes my dreams.

'I'm very flattered. Truly, I am.' He smiles warmly, but words fail us. What else is there to say?

The fairy tale is over.

Kings and queens twirl around me, smiling and laughing, as music plays on under the starry lights above. I am caught in the eye of their perfect storm and want the ground to swallow me whole.

The compere's announcement snaps me back to reality, and Mrs Life-and-Soul grabs Prince Charming's hand and whisks him off to the dance floor. Shaking to my very core, I push my way through the crowd in a daze. I snatch champagne from a passing tray and immediately down it before escaping into the night.

The fresh breeze hits my burning cheeks, while each falling tear pricks with humiliation. Gathering my skirts, I flee down the stairs as fast as my ridiculous heels allow. As I run across the lawn towards the woods, a pointed toe catches in the flowing fabric that rips as I skid on the grass. Unable to keep my balance, I tumble to the ground, hearing more tearing as I land on my hands and knees.

My head is swimming, sinking. I'm drowning, my chest so tight against my bodice that I can't breathe. My carefully pinned curls fall and unravel. I must keep going. Here is not the place to fall apart.

Looking as undignified as I feel, I clamber to my feet and, with a muddied hand, push the hair from my face, knocking the rose to the ground. A heel has snapped off one of my new shoes. I kick them off and run onwards with bare feet.

Finally out of sight from the throng, I sink behind a tree and release the flood of unrelenting tears.

Pain sears through my chest as the dreams I had built come tumbling down. Grieving for what could have been, I hold my head in my hands. I'm in limbo, suspended in a surreal blur of how to process the no I hadn't expected to hear, the no I don't want to accept. I don't want this to be the end. It can't be the end. I am raw, the pain too much to bear.

Why did I do this to myself? What a fool to become swept up in such fantasy. At my age. Allowing myself to be lured by a romantic dream of a young, handsome Prince Charming – who was just playing a role, doing his job.

Who was I kidding? I'm just a middle-aged mum seeking a little happiness. I'm not a cougar or some brazen hussy. OK, I was brazen, this once. I made a mistake, never, ever to be repeated. Ever.

My husband doesn't want me – how did I ever convince myself that Jisung might want me, even for a single night?

Tears of self-pity flow freely, hot and stinging, as gut-wrenching shame rises like bile in my throat. I feel stripped bare, as if all my flaws and failings are on full display. As though a lifetime of never feeling like I'm enough, of constantly shrinking from mirrors and obsessing over every imperfection, suddenly comes flooding to the forefront until I'm drowning in self-doubt.

I claw at my hair, nails raking my scalp, as self-loathing courses through my veins like poison. The urge to scream builds in my chest, fighting to erupt from my lips. I rip handfuls of grass from its roots and pummel the ground with my palms, relishing the dull pain that matches the ache in my chest. The rough bark of the tree digs into my back, the canopy of leaves overhead bending and blurring through the haze of tears that won't stop flowing. I roll onto my knees and dry retch.

I have to get away. I need to hide. I know I have to get back to my room and remove this elegant facade.

Scrambling to my feet, I rub my sore eyes dry, sobs clogging my throat. I look down at my poor ripped and muddy gown, wincing in shame. My self-esteem as tattered as my dress.

My reality is broken and my fantasy crushed. I must be the only person to try – and fail – to have an affair. I'm an idiot and a failure. I am empty, my body drained. I am done.

Somehow, I eventually summon the strength to go back to the hotel, desperately hoping no one sees me in this state – especially not Lexi.

But as I turn, I see Jisung running in my direction. I cower back behind the tree, holding my breath, praying he hasn't seen me. He calls my name. I squeeze my eyes closed, wishing I could disappear.

A hand grips my arm, startling me. 'Cally, what's wrong?' Jisung asks urgently. I force my eyes open and glance up at his alarmed face. He wraps his coat around me, and must notice the red marks marring my skin. 'You're hurt.' His fingertips softly trace the scratches. 'What happened?'

Unable to meet his searching gaze, I stare down, deeply aware that I look rather more dishevelled than when he saw me last.

He holds out the rose and shoes left scattered on the grass. 'I was so worried,' he admits, his voice gentle and soothing.

'I'm fine,' I croak, taking them from his hand and then dropping them to the ground again. 'I'm sorry.' My body slumps, overcome with guilt.

He gently puts his hand on my shoulder. 'You have nothing to apologise for.'

'I'm sorry for being crazy and putting you in that awkward position.' My voice breaks and another tear escapes.

'Shh, it's OK,' he whispers, comforting me as I sob. 'You're not crazy, Cally. You're hurting. Let me help you.'

Reaching into his breast pocket, he pulls out a handkerchief and wipes away my tears, gently rubbing at the mascara and mud dried on my cheeks. He puts the silky cloth to my nose and murmurs, 'Blow.'

'I get it. It wasn't real. You were just doing your job.'

'No, Cally, let me explain.' He lifts my chin until our eyes meet, then takes hold of my shoulders.

'I like you. A lot. I want nothing more than to throw you on my bed and treat you to a night of passion.'

My exhausted brain struggles to grasp his words. My knees tremble, and he holds me more firmly.

'You aren't the only one to be tempted here tonight,' he says with a bittersweet smile. 'My heart doesn't always obey the rules either.' The smile fades from his lips.

'But we can't.' His eyes are full of sadness; his voice is low and pained. 'You are married and confused. Regret is the most painful thing in life. I don't want to be a mistake that causes you pain.' He breaks off, and a frown darkens his face as he quietly adds, 'And... I don't want to get hurt.'

My head falls as I accept Jisung's words. I hate someone making a decision for me, but I know deep down that he is right. I hate having to be sensible when I want to be reckless and carefree. But most of all, I hate that I've lost myself.

I look back up at this wonderful man who is looking after my best interests.

'I understand. There's no happy ending for us,' I rasp, my heart heavy with desperate sadness. His solemn expression melts into a warm smile, his head cocked to one side.

'But we can be happy together in this moment. Come with me.'

Gazebo

Moonlight filters through the dense canopy above as Jisung leads me by the hand through the shadowed forest. When we emerge into a secluded glen, there before us lies a hidden treasure – an old stone gazebo. Twinkling fairy lights illuminate the domed roof and trail down its pillars, setting the night aglow.

'My lady, shall we finish our dance?'

Surrounded by the glimmering lights, he looks like a dream. Here, right now, he is still my Prince Charming. 'I would love to.'

He leads me up the crooked steps to our dancefloor and grabs me, twirling me round and round. The world spins, and we tumble into a giggling heap. Laughter releases the tension.

Feeling flushed, I let his coat slip to the floor and he pulls me up to my feet. I straighten my bodice and rest against a cool stone pillar to steady my breath.

Jisung approaches from behind and curls his arms around me in our first, and maybe last, hug. We stand in silence, watching the last of the beautiful tangerine-and-cherry sunset succumb to the darkness. For now at least, I find solace in his arms.

He nuzzles into my neck and gives a long, sorrowful sigh. In that moment, I see this from his eyes for the first time; the impossibility of our situation can't be easy for him, either. My heart swells with tenderness for this man who is being strong enough for both of us. Lesser men might have taken the easy option without a second thought of the consequences.

'I never needed anything from you, Jisung. I just wanted to spend time with you. For you to see me – as Cally, not as Cally the mum, or wife, or reporter. I wanted to feel like... me again.' I turn in his arms to face him, blinking back tears.

'I understand. You want to be treated as you deserve, appreciated as the strong, independent, sexy woman you are.' He slides his hand down my side – over the curves of my waist and hips. I laugh and lightly slap his hand, feeling self-conscious. I'm stunned to hear his words when such thoughts of myself have long faded. But Jisung thinking of me in this way is the greatest affirmation I could receive and makes me consider that maybe his words could hold some truth.

'I'm right though, yes?' he questions sincerely. He drops his head to meet my eye level. 'Yes?'

'Maybe,' I mumble.

Well, that's a first. I just acknowledged I have needs. Needs of my own, purely for me.

'We all have needs,' he says, as though reading my thoughts. He brushes a lock of hair from my eyes, his fingers lingering on my cheek. 'You deserve so much, Cally. You deserve to be happy.' His voice is thick with emotion. 'You're special to me.'

I melt in his arms, and we hold each other close. 'You'll get through this. I believe in you.' He leans down, his cheek pressed against mine, and whispers, 'My Princess Badass.' We both burst out laughing, and I squeal as he lifts me up and spins me around.

We stay a while holding each other, swaying to the hush of whispering leaves. I lean into his comforting touch as he holds my head to his chest, stroking my hair, and I breathe in the scent of his skin. 'Do you think Lexi will forgive me for not being with her at the ball?'

'Cally, I've seen the two of you together this week. You're her world. She is a real credit to you, and you are a wonderful mum.'

My bottom lip trembles and my eyes well up once again. 'That's very kind of you to say. I'll have to make it up to her in the morning... our last morning.' I clutch him tightly, a tight knot burning in my stomach. 'I don't want to leave you.'

He places his hand softly on my cheek and looks into my eyes. 'I'm not going anywhere.'

My eyes fly wide open at his words, and my body stiffens with a terrifying realisation. 'Next week you'll be someone else's Prince Charming.' He'll sweep some other woman off her feet. He'll flash that charming smile, make her feel like the only woman in the world. The way he's made me feel. My chest constricts and fear floods the hollowness inside. My shaking hands clutch his arms, and I search his face desperately.

'No!' he says in earnest, gripping my waist. 'I've never... I would never... it's only you.' His voice is raised, speech rapid. 'I know it's fast and seems crazy, and I can't explain it.' He pulls me urgently to him. 'But I feel it inside, a special connection.'

'I don't want to leave you,' I whisper, choking back tears. How can I feel so insanely happy and desperately sad at the same time? I look up to see him wiping away a tear, and he pulls my head back to his chest. 'We will always have the time we spent together.'

We cling to each other as though we're both wondering where the hell we go from here, even though I think we both know deep down. Eventually, he releases a long sigh and my body softens. We spend a while taking deep breaths, and I feel his heartbeat slowing.

With a shift in his energy, he kisses the top of my head and slowly pulls away. 'Cally, the feelings I have for you are real.' He takes a step back but keeps my hands folded in his own, looking deep into my eyes. 'You bring colour to my days and make me smile again. I like who I am when I'm with you.' He looks away, running his fingers through his hair. 'There are too many obstacles right now. But life has a way of clearing the path when the time is right.' His eyes find mine again, deep with meaning. 'We never know what the future may hold.'

His words gift me the glimmer of hope I need to take home, to hold like fireflies in a jar, lighting my path ahead. 'Meeting you has made me clearer than ever. I feel strong enough now to do whatever it takes.'

He squeezes my hands and smiles gently. 'We need to go.' His voice is soft and tinged with sadness. I sigh, long and hard, and brush his smooth cheek with my fingertips.

'I need to make preparations for tomorrow, and you... need a shower. You're filthy.' He holds up my palm, and we laugh at the mud caked up my arms.

'Come.' He collects his coat and puts it back around my shoulders, offering to carry me to the hotel. I shake my head and gather my skirts in both hands. With his arm around my waist, we begin a slow, careful walk back to the hotel.

As we leave the sanctuary of the gazebo, a wave of sadness washes over me. Our perfect escape is at an end, and with it my dreams.

He grabs my shoes along the way – my new bag was lost long ago. Oh, with my wedding ring inside. I don't think the universe could send a clearer sign.

My bare feet are grateful it's mostly soft grass all the way, even if it is damp and cold. It's a quiet stroll, calm after the emotional storm of the evening. My mind and body are drained and long for the relief of sleep.

Bright lights and laughter spill from the hotel windows, stinging my eyes as we approach the steps. Jisung stops and sweeps me up into his arms. I throw my arms around his shoulders and cling to his waistcoat, but he doesn't even break into a sweat and lifts me with ease. Feeling safe, I snuggle into his warm neck as he carries me up the stairs and inside the door.

Diane flies over to us in a frenzy of concerned cries. 'My poor girl, what on earth has happened to you?' She throws her hands in the air, looking utterly horrified. Jisung lowers me to the ground.

'I'm fine, please don't worry.' I place a reassuring hand on her shoulder. Admittedly, I look far from fine. 'I just fell over. I'm OK, I promise.'

She fusses around me. 'Let me help you to your room.'

Mine and Jisung's fingers untwine as she ushers me towards the elevator. I have barely enough time to mouth goodbye to him before Diane gathers my skirts and bundles me into the lift.

As the doors close, he calls, 'Meet me in the courtyard at midday.'

SUNDAY

Happily Ever After?

I wake at an unearthly hour and bury my head under the security of the duvet; our last day can't begin until I open my eyes. And I definitely can't panic about work until I've had coffee. Cosy and warm, I lie quietly with my thoughts. What a holiday!

My whole life has turned upside down and inside out. This week's emotional turmoil has been the jolt I didn't know I needed, and meeting Jisung was the wake-up call to all the possibilities I had closed myself to. And now there's no going back. I can't return to the same way of life. I don't want to settle for second best anymore – Lexi and I both deserve more.

I don't have all the details figured out for the future, and I know I may lose my way, but right now Jisung is the sunshine that gives me hope, and every inch of me aches to be with him today. I also know this promotion and pay rise is more important than ever if I'm to make changes for mine and Lexi's happiness. And I haven't made any progress with writing my review.

But Lexi is my priority. I want to make every effort to be a better mum, and I want to show her she is my everything.

'Mum? You over there?' Lexi's voice sounds muffled behind the curtain.

'Of course, baby.'

'Where were you? I couldn't see you.'

'I know... I'm so sorry. Come and have a snuggle.' I am wracked with more guilt than I want to feel again. On the last night of our once-in-a-lifetime holiday, the ball should have been the highlight of the fairy-tale week we shared together.

Lexi clambers over my bed and wriggles under the covers.

'Did you have fun, Lex?'

'I didn't get to see your dress.' She lets me pull her into a cuddle. 'But the carriage ride was awesome! And I danced with Baby Bear! Can I do dance lessons when we go home? And singing and acting? I want to join the cast when I'm old enough.'

'I'm sure we can arrange that.' I squeeze her tight. 'I really am sorry I missed it, but I'm so glad I saw your performance. How can I make it up to you?'

Lexi pulls funny faces while she thinks, ending with a mischievous grin. 'I know... ice cream for breakfast!' We both giggle.

'It's a deal!' That was easier than I feared. She has a sweet, forgiving heart. 'Let's pack our cases quick and go for ice cream.'

Seems there's nothing like the promise of ice cream to motivate Lexi into speed-packing. In no time, her belongings are packed, the bathroom is emptied of its freebies, the ballgown is zipped in its bag, and Princess Bear is ready to board the bus. I'm unsure whether to pack my torn ballgown, especially with the memories it holds. I save the decision for later, put Nanny P's gift in my handbag, and we're ready for our ice cream hunt.

As we leave the bedroom, I narrowly avoid stepping on a single red rose left outside our door, like the one Jisung gave me last night. White rose petals are scattered to form an arrow, and a confetti trail leads along the corridor. Lexi and I look at each other, both bewildered and thrilled.

Eyes alight, Lexi skips alongside the petals. 'It's a treasure hunt!'

Her delight is as contagious as always, and we set off to discover whatever treat lies in store.

We follow the confetti out of the hotel and across the grass towards the woods. We pass bellboys ferrying luggage while guests roam the resort, a few looking worse for wear as they struggle to keep up with their kids' energy. It appears this intriguing trail is just for us! A final adventure for the journalist to review, perhaps?

'Look, Mum! Over there!' Lexi points to a red rose as tall as me, showing where the path goes through the trees.

Within the dark woods, giant poppies and golden sunflowers line the route, each glowing brightly to light our way. The musky scent of rich, damp earth envelops us as we continue past a familiar gazebo. For a moment, its twinkles pull me back to last night, secure in Jisung's arms.

Soon we pass enormous luminescent mushrooms, each bigger than the last. Lexi twirls beneath the glow of a great sunflower, her laughter echoing through the trees. 'I wish we lived here. I would never get bored of magic surprises.' She grabs my hand as we walk excitedly to the wood's edge to discover what lies beyond.

The trees give way to thick, lush planting along a drystone wall. There in front of us, the stones form a circular passageway through a gravity-defying moon gate. Lexi and I stand in the magical portal and stare in disbelief and awe. Her fingers twining in mine, she draws me into this secret world meant for our delight alone.

Here, the trail ends. A magnificent garden of towering sunflowers and daisies beckons, with huge sculptures of butterflies, toadstools, and great dandelion blowballs. A blanket strewn with cushions lays in the centre of the lawn. A hamper invites us to picnic and play with a stack of board games.

Someone has gone to extreme lengths to prepare the most astounding occasion for us.

As we get closer, we read the signpost:

For Lexi and Cally, with love x

The wooden stump stuck in the ground features the small giveaway – Prince Charming's circle of gold wax stamped with the initials PC. My heart flutters at the sight. Jisung? I am stunned – never before has anyone made this much effort to make me feel special. Jisung is one of a kind.

Lexi and I dive into our picnic feast, and although there is no ice cream, there are plenty of other inappropriate breakfast items, much to Lexi's delight. We are tempted by pink candy apples topped with doughnuts and swirls of fondant and sprinkles, and a bouquet of pink and white cake pops. Although from what I've seen of the resort's catering, the homemade goodies likely contain a dozen hidden fruits and vegetables masquerading as a sugar rush. I'm most grateful for the coffee. We both find the plate of lettuce a rather odd offering, opting instead for delicious fruit scones with jam and clotted cream.

We while away a couple of sublime hours in the morning sun. We play cards and complete a jigsaw together – things we rarely find time to do anymore. We play on the tree swings and collapse in giggles when making many unsuccessful attempts to climb in the hammock. It is wonderful to spend this undisturbed time with Lexi, without the usual distractions of electronic devices and chores.

'Mum!' Lexi gasps and points to the beds of my favourite aquilegia flowers.

'Pretty, aren't they?'

'Shhhhh! No, Mum, I saw a bunny!'

We stay very still and quiet, attentive to any rustling or signs of movement.

Then, a flash of white – two grey bunnies emerge, velvet coats glinting silver in the dappled light. Cautious, quivering noses testing the air, ears pricked forward, they venture closer to Lexi's feet.

I subtly point to the lettuce, mouthing for Lexi to hold out a leaf. Heart in my throat, I watch as one nibbles from her trembling fingers, whiskers softly brushing her

skin. Lexi can barely control her excitement. For urban-
ites like us, this moment is pure magic, and I understand
why this garden was chosen for our special treat. Jisung's
gift will stay etched in our memories.

We've been thoroughly spoiled this week, and now,
with time running short, it's our turn to treat someone else.

'Shall we pack up and find Nanny P?'

'I'm going to miss her.' Lexi rubs her eyes, trying to
keep her tears at bay.

'Me too.' I put my arms around my sad little girl for
a big cuddle. 'I bought her a present. Would you like to
give it to her?'

'Yes! Yes, please.'

I tidy away the games while Lexi bundles a heap of
candy jewellery into my bag.

'Bye, bunnies! Thank you for coming to our tea party,' Lexi calls out to the bushes. She takes my hand, ready
to follow the confetti trail back to the hotel. She looks
up at me with cute puppy eyes and, in the sweetest voice,
says, 'Mummy... please could we get a pet bunny when
we get home?'

***

Lexi spots Nanny P near the magic tree and runs to her
with open arms, gift in hand. They're still nestled close
when I finally catch up.

'I was worried I'd missed you.' Nanny P pulls me into
a group hug. I squeeze her hand. 'Thank you so much for
everything this week. You are an angel.'

'It's been my pleasure. I've loved spending time with Lexi.' Nanny P twiddles with Lexi's curls, and Lexi looks up at her adoringly. 'We've got you a present!'

'Ooh! You shouldn't have.' Nanny P's cheeks become rosier, and her eyes look a little misty. Lexi gives her the biggest smile, then slowly turns her head towards me.

'Muuum?'

I inwardly laugh, wondering what she wants now... Two bunnies? Her own petting zoo? To smuggle Nanny P in her suitcase to take home? 'Ye-es?'

'Please could we go to the Little Pigs' Party so I can say goodbye to my friends?' Lexi has perfected her pleading eye look with fluttering eyelashes that are impossible to resist.

I check the clock on my phone and smile. We have enough time. Lexi jumps around in a frenzy of twirls and squeals all the way to the party, keeping Nanny P and I in fits of giggles.

Lexi runs to join her friends, who are mid-way through building a house made of straw, screaming with laughter at the three pigs' antics. Nanny P joins in their game, while I find a bench amongst the flowers.

As I sit in this sunny paradise, watching my daughter have the time of her life, my chest shudders inside and my eyes well with tears. Leaving our magical holiday feels more like we're being torn from home, and I know a piece of my heart will be left behind. If it wasn't for my precious Barney dog, there would be nothing to return to. And that's before I even consider *who* I'm leaving behind.

Just that brief thought is surreal and like a punch to the chest. I can't allow myself to think about that now. I can't break down in front of the kids.

I stroll over to the drinks cart to take my mind off the pain with the squeals and laughter of children ringing in my ears. I spot the snout of a wolf peeking through the hedges and laugh, knowing the thrills he's about to cause. As I pour myself a glass of juice, my shoulders are already beginning to stiffen, ready to return to their stressed hunch of home.

Before I go back to my bench, I stop and take a moment to smell some of the beautiful flowers. Their fragrance is soothing, and I take some slow breaths to try and recapture the calm this place brings. I close my eyes and simply listen to the sounds of joy. Those become the screams of playful terror, so I assume the wolf has made his entrance.

As I wander towards the bench, phrases come to mind about our extraordinary experiences here. The enchantment right from when we arrived, the idyllic landscape, the opulence of the fairy-tale palace hotel. I run to the bench to take out my notebook. I have to write these phrases down as they form into sentences, before the ideas float away to wherever they came from.

I write non-stop, pausing only to think of the right word or reflect on our wonderful memories and the staff I've grown so fond of and all they've done for me and Lexi. My pen speeds across the page, writing whatever comes to mind, words that describe the feelings that staying here evokes. The magic, the joy, the connection. And there's only one word I can use for the perfect ending.

When I put down my pen, I sit back, almost out of breath, and look up at the sky to the solitary wispy cloud. My chest rises in a satisfied sigh. I've bloody done it! The first draft of my review is complete! All the worry is lifted, my body feels lighter, and my head feels high with a sense of achievement.

First Draft

Fairy-Tale Wonderland

A Review

by Cally Jackson

From the moment of arrival at the enchanting entrance to Fairy-Tale Wonderland, I was transported to a world of childhood wonder and nostalgia. The whimsical atmosphere evokes memories of childhood fantasies of beautiful princesses, heroic rescues by *(breathtakingly handsome)* princes, brave knights defeating dragons, and finding your one true love. *(Sigh)*

Centred in the idyllic landscape, the magnificent fairy-tale palace hotel exudes opulence, and its restaurants offer exquisite culinary adventures *(maybe avoid chocolate pancakes though)*. Top chefs create delicious and imaginatively presented dishes that are *(miraculously)* devoured by even the fussiest of little mouths.

But at the very heart of Fairy-Tale Wonderland is the pure joy of reconnecting with the love of your family and cherishing every moment to create priceless, once-in-a-lifetime memories.

With a delightful array of activities available to relax, unwind, and play, each family can create their dream holiday. The staff *(apart from Todgers)* are attentive and professional, ensuring that guests' every need is met *(even when you're a rude, spoilt brat)*, making for a truly un-forgettable experience.

Whether joining the resort's cast of characters for a full schedule of family entertainment, exploring the mes-merising grounds for hidden treasures, or taking a little time out to relax in the spa *(preferably without drown-ing)*, both parents and children are given the chance to live out their fairy-tale dreams.

During my stay, the colourful and fragrant flower gardens rekindled an appreciation of the beauty and peace of nature, and the maze *(from hell, grrr)* of stepping-stone pathways was a reminder of the endless possibilities that arrive with each new dawn.

Enjoying such fun and laughter with my daughter, I discovered that we are never too old for fairy-tales, and a sprinkle of the resort's magic made me feel like a princess in my own story *(with my own gorgeous Prince Charming)*. Before our holiday was even over, I was dreaming of our return. But the most precious moment of all was realising that true love's kisses come from your own children.

This luxurious and unique resort offers the ultimate in magical five-star experiences that are the perfect start of your family's own happily ever after. *(And I can't wait!!!)*

Fairy-Tale Wonderland is, quite simply, spectacular.

***

Just a few edits and it will be a piece I can be proud to put my name to. I stand up to stretch my back and shoulders, lost in my speeding thoughts. I can't believe how that just happened, how I was suddenly hit by inspiration and the words just flowed. I close my eyes and roll my neck, feeling the relief of stretching out tight muscles.

When I open my eyes, I notice the children carrying foam bricks, which must mean their games are soon coming to an end. I check the time and have an instant hot flush and let out a groan. Why am I always running late? I jog over to Nanny P.

'Please could you watch Lexi one last time while I quickly sort our luggage?'

'Absolutely!' she replies with her lovely warm smile.

I leave the gift on the bench, leave the happy duo to their games, and rush to our room. The bus leaves in thirty minutes. I'm cutting it fine. I take the elevator and run down the corridor.

Our room sits hollow, cases whisked away. At least that settles the dress dilemma. But Prince Charming's coat, still round my shoulders last night, is nowhere in sight. It must have been loaded onto the bus. I can't inadvertently steal his costume.

Snap decision made, I dash down to the hotel shop. A customer is being served. The assistant plods along, wrapping at a snail's pace as minutes bleed away. I hop from foot to foot, too worried about the time ticking by to marvel at the magical wares. I hop faster, wondering if I should step in and pack the customer's items myself.

Eventually, it's my turn to be served. Unsurprisingly, the assistant doesn't understand why I want to buy Prince Charming a coat, and I have to waste too much valuable time explaining. But I finally manage to order the coat and a replacement handkerchief, and have the sudden inspiration to get the handkerchief embroidered with a little message:

Always remember

You are priceless

And unforgettable

***

Jisung casually leans against the table at the far end of the private courtyard. A vision of perfection in a black leather jacket and ripped black jeans. The sun casts a warm glow over his beautiful face, and his eyes light up when he sees me. I can't bear the thought of never seeing him again. It doesn't feel real. I don't want it to be real.

My heart is pounding as I run to him, not wanting to waste a precious second.

'I don't have long.'

He takes a step towards me. 'Our last chance to be alone.' He's as cool as ever, but there is sadness in his eyes.

He reaches inside his jacket and pulls out a small box tied with a pink ribbon, holding it out to me without saying a word. My heart beats even faster and my fingers tremble as I reach for the gift. 'For me?'

He nods, a shy smile tugging at his lips. Heart fluttering, I untie the bow with care and lift the lid to find a mushroom house bracelet! My hand flies to my open mouth in genuine surprise, and my stomach flips.

I blink back tears as I gaze at the tiny wooden pendant, my fingers running over the intricately carved windows and door. 'Our house! Just as I imagined it. It's beautiful, thank you.' I look up at Jisung, wanting to remember every single detail of his handsome face.

He takes the bracelet out of the box and fixes it around my wrist with a smile. 'A perfect fit. Now wherever you go, I can be by your side.' He kisses my hand and holds it over his heart. 'Don't forget me.'

He gently holds my hands and we stare into each other's eyes. My heart shatters, and I can barely breathe.

'I could never forget you, my Prince Charming.' Breath shuddering, I grip his hands hard, never wanting to let go. He wipes away a tear that has escaped down my cheek and places his hand on the back of my head, the other pulling me close. I grip him tightly and rest my head on his chest.

My own chest quivers as I try to hold myself together. Life is so cruel to introduce me to someone who could be my one chance of true happiness, my one and only true love, and then snatch them away.

'We never got to wish on the shooting star firework.' My lips tremble. 'My wish is that I could hold you forever.' I bury my face in his chest. I breathe him in like air, commit the feel of his arms around me to memory.

Even though my heart clings tight to a tiny shred of hope, pain sears through my stomach. I know it's our last goodbye.

He pulls back, his arms still around my shoulders, and lightly kisses my forehead. His eyes look red and watery, which makes me swallow hard, trying to hold back my tears. He caresses my cheek with such affection in his face. 'Let's look back at happy memories, not sad endings. No final words, OK?'

I nod and try to smile. I don't want his last memory of me to be ugly crying. My hands slip from his waist.

It's time.

I force myself to turn. It takes everything I have to force my feet to move in the direction of the exit. My insides are in pieces, and my chest aches with every step further from him. I am desperate to turn around and run back into his arms. I'm not sure how I'm going to do this. How do you walk away from someone when your heart is begging you to stay?

But I have to leave.

I dry my eyes on my sleeve, take a deep breath, and slowly walk away.

I steal one last glance at my fairy tale. He is standing in the same spot, hands in his jeans pockets. He winks and flashes his beautiful eye-crinkling smile, making me as giddy as the first time I saw him.

Grateful to have met him, thankful for the magical moments we shared, I am able to give a happy smile as I slowly turn back to face reality.

***

Although I may not have got my prince, my shattered heart continues to beat. I will go on with hope now that

I have begun to get *me* back. The strong, fun Cally I was before an unfulfilling marriage took its toll. The Cally who has needs and is special and deserves happiness. The badass who will cope with the difficult path ahead to create her own happy ending.

As I turn the corner onto the narrow path from the courtyard, Jisung's voice calls out, 'Wait!' He grabs my arm from behind, spinning me back into his arms, lips capturing mine. He takes my breath away. My eyes are wide in surprise, heart hammering in my chest, although my body instinctively wilts into his embrace.

He cups my face and kisses me firmly, urgently. His lips are soft and warm, the taste of him intoxicating. He wraps his arms around me and I reach inside his jacket to hold him tight. Closing my eyes, I return his kiss, gently, slowly, fully giving myself to him. His tongue runs along my lip, sparking a voracious, insatiable passion between us.

The world falls away until nothing exists but this – his kiss, hungry and deep, and the feel of him holding me together as I come undone. My whole being is focused on the sensation of his lips on mine, his hands on my skin, and the way our bodies fit perfectly together. Heat courses through me everywhere we touch.

I drown in the taste of him. His kiss is everything I have imagined and more. I stroke his cheek and run my fingers through his hair while he covers my lips in light, fluttery kisses in between our smiles.

How I wish time would stand still so he could throw me on his bed for that night of passion.

'Cally, I may not be your first kiss, but I would be honoured to be your last.'

His smile hides the tears he's fighting. He kisses my cheek one last time. 'My only wish... that one day you'll come back to me.'

SUNDAY

One Way Or Another

Heading to the resort exit, I reach the book gateway that was our first experience of this Fairy-Tale Wonderland – only a week ago, when I was weary and closed off. And now I leave, exhilarated and happily exhausted from a week of learning how to fully live again.

The magical book opens to reveal its arched exit and reads:

And they lived happily ever after...

As I pass through and head towards home, my heart whispers in return: *We will.*

I climb aboard the bus and float down the aisle, lips still zinging. I pass Mrs Life-and-Soul, who takes one look at my red, puffy eyes and nods. 'You'll be back.'

Lexi is flicking through the memories captured on the pages of our new photo book, a huge smile on her face. She glances up as I sit next to her. 'Aww, don't be sad, Mum. We can play princesses at home, if you like? Here, have some of my orange soda.'

I rest my head back and close my eyes; I have one very last thing to do before we head away.

Are you there, Universe? It's me, Cally. I am wishing on every star in the galaxy, cosmic manifesting, appealing to the law of attraction, law of gravity, relativity, Pythagoras... please let me return to my wonderland.

One way or another, I'm determined to go back.

To be continued...

The Story Continues...

Snuggle up and indulge in some *me time* (champagne optional) as you embark on the next part of Cally's journey in Happily Ever After?

Follow along as Cally returns to the enchanting Fairy Tale Wonderland at the most magical time of the year – Christmas! Will the spirit of the season be enough to make Cally's dreams come true? Will she find her perfect fairy tale ending with Prince Charming?

With all the humour and hijinks you loved in Never Too Old For Fairy Tales, this sequel promises another whimsical escape full of friendship, festivities, and fairy tale romance.

Order your copy of **Happily Ever After?** from Amazon
bit.ly/Cally2

Dear Lovely Reader

Thank you for joining me in the enchanting world of *Never Too Old for Fairy Tales*. It was such fun to write and I hope you enjoyed escaping into the whimsical world of Fairy Tale Wonderland.

I'm thrilled to announce that Cally is returning for a winter wonderland adventure in *Happily Ever After?* Prepare to be delighted by this heartwarming sequel full of Christmas magic! I can't wait for you to join Cally on her quest for a second chance with Prince Charming.

Thank you once again for your support and for allowing me to share my story with you. I hope to connect with you soon.

Warmest regards
Melissa

Ps. Your feedback means the world to me. I would love to hear what you liked about *Never Too Old for Fairy Tales*, and it would be great if you could leave a review on Amazon or Goodreads. Your kind words will help other readers discover their chance to fall in love with Prince Charming too – and allow me to keep writing!

Acknowledgements

Behind the scenes of every book is a community of support. I couldn't have done this without *my people*, and I am truly grateful.

With special thanks to:
Amy, Annie, Dana, Ellie, Jackie, Jennifer, Laura, Marie, Mumma, Rachel, and Yvonne.

Chloe Cran, my wonderful editor. You are an angel.

Author Bio

I'm Melissa John, a British writer and 40-something mum, inspired by my obsessive fangirling over Kpop and KDrama, and with a passion for escaping into enchanting worlds of whimsy and romance. I love to write heart-warming stories for women in midlife who follow their dreams to create their own happy endings.

Email
melissa@melissajohn.co.uk
Facebook
melissajohnauthor
Instagram
@melissajohnauthor

Reader Bonus

Immerse yourself in the enchanting visuals that breathe life into each chapter of *Never Too Old for Fairy Tales*. Explore the captivating imagery, let your imagination soar, and embark on a delightful visual adventure through this curated Pinterest board.

Pinterest
bit.ly/PinNTOFFT

Printed in Great Britain
by Amazon

29888127R00148